As they crested the ridge, he saw more than fifty men, all bearing flaming torches and armed with a hodgepodge of farm implements. From his vantage point, Theo could see pitchforks, shovels, pickaxes, and even something that might have been a cricket bat silhouetted against the flickering orange light.

As he stared in mounting horror, a harsh voice that could only have belonged to Abel Wilkins bellowed, "Are you with me?"

The assembled men shouted their assent.

"To the mill, then!"

"To the mill!" echoed the men, and the torches bobbed crazily against the night sky as the group set out toward the road that led to the village and the cotton mill beyond.

"Good God!" Theo stared down at Daphne, his eyes glittering in the feeble light. "They're marching on the mill! I've got to stop them!"

She clung to his sleeve. "Mr. Tisdale—Theo—you will be careful, won't you?"

Theo had already begun to turn away, but at this entreaty he stopped, seized her by the arms, and kissed her swift and hard on the mouth. The kiss was over almost as soon as it began, but when he would have released her, she flung her arms about his neck and kissed him back with all the love and passion and fear she could never put into words.

The Desperate Duke

Sheri Cobb South

1

Bury the Great Duke
With an empire's lamentation.
ALFRED, LORD TENNYSON,
Ode on the Death of the Duke of Wellington

October 1820
Reddington Hall, Devon

The Duke of Reddington was dying. Granted, the physician had not put it quite so bluntly, but upon being castigated by his aristocratic patient as a mealy-mouthed old woman and commanded to give said patient the truth with no bark upon it, Dr. Donald Grant (Edinburgh-trained, and having temporarily forsaken his thriving Harley Street practice for the express purpose of attending his grace) was perhaps understandably goaded into informing the duke that his life might henceforth be more accurately measured in days than years. Theodore, Viscount Tisdale—his grace's son and heir—was duly summoned from his bachelor flat in London's Albany; likewise, the duke's daughter and her husband were also sent for. As these latter were obliged to travel from Lancashire over indifferent roads, it was generally felt by the duke's household staff that Lady Helen and Sir Ethan Brundy would in all likelihood arrive too late for Lady Helen to bid her father farewell. But as if bent upon proving them wrong out of sheer contrariness (no one entertained for even a moment the possibility that his determination to live might be inspired by affection for his elder child), his grace was still clinging to life four days later, when Sir Ethan Brundy's well-sprung but sadly mud-splattered carriage lurched to a stop before the portico of Reddington Hall.

The great front door was flung open, and a liveried footman came running out of the house with an umbrella to hold over their heads.

"Welcome home, my lady. How do you do, Sir Ethan?" the butler intoned with sober dignity, in the hushed tones he considered appropriate to the occasion.

"Thank you, Figgins. How do you do?" Lady Helen asked as she divested herself of her rain-dappled pelisse. "And how is Mrs. Figgins?"

"Quite well, my lady," he responded with a hint of impatience, dismissing the health of both himself and his wife as a matter of no importance as he received Sir Ethan's damp greatcoat, hat, and gloves. "It is good of you to ask. Alas, your father, I fear—"

He got no further before Viscount Tisdale entered the hall, boot heels ringing against the marble-tiled floor.

"Nell!" Theodore exclaimed, white-faced. "Thank God you've come. You too, Ethan," he added, nodding at his brother-in-law over his sister's shoulder as he enveloped her in a brotherly embrace.

"We came as soon as we got word, Teddy," she assured him. "But is Papa so very bad, then? I thought perhaps it was no more than one of his distempered freaks."

It would not have been the first time in the four years since her marriage that she had received an urgent summons to her father's bedside, only to discover that there was nothing the matter with him that an infusion of funds from her husband's bank account could not cure.

"I think he may be for it this time," the viscount confided, lowering his voice as if their father might hear the conversation from his bedchamber two floors above. "Dr. Grant says so, although Papa abused him like a pickpocket for it. Still, I've never seen Papa so—so—but come upstairs, and you can see for yourself."

Lady Helen needed no urging. She dumped her pelisse into Figgins's arms and made for the stairs, her husband at her heels and her brother at her side.

"Grant says it's his heart," Theodore continued as they climbed the broad staircase side by side, with Sir Ethan bringing up the rear. "He's been in a rare taking ever since—well—"

"Ever since he'd discovered you had that female in keeping," his sister concluded sagely. "What do they call her? La Fantasia, isn't it?"

Theodore gave his sister a rather sheepish look. "Oh, so you know about that, do you?"

Lady Helen made a noise that, in a lesser female, would

have been called a snort. "Can you wonder at it? When you will insist upon appearing in the park or at the theatre with the creature on your arm, you can't suppose that any number of my London acquaintances won't write to me—all in the greatest concern, of course!—to tell me that my brother has taken up with a regular high-flyer. Really, Teddy, you might at least try for a little discretion!"

"You sound just like Papa," the viscount grumbled, forgetting for the moment the fragile state of his father's health. "Lord, you never heard such a fuss! You'd think he'd been a monk in his younger days—which he wasn't, not if half the stories he's let slip while in his cups were true, let me tell you!"

"Of course not, but Papa is always flying up into the boughs over something. Depend upon it, he'll come about, once he sees he can't—"

She broke off as he opened the door to the duke's bedchamber. The indefinable odor of the sickroom met them, along with a wall of heat, for the fire in the grate had been stirred to a blaze. The doctor, sweat running down his face, looked up at their entrance.

"Ah, how do you do, Lady Helen, Sir Ethan? So pleased you could make it in time, er, that is, I'm sure you'll want a word alone with his grace, so I'll just step outside, shall I? If he should take a sudden turn for the worse, I'll not be far away."

Suiting the word to the deed, he quitted the room, leaving the black bag that held the accoutrements of his profession standing on the small table at the duke's bedside. Clearly, he did not expect to be long absent from the sickroom.

Lady Helen advanced into the room, saying, "What's all this, Papa? Has Teddy been plaguing—" Her voice faltered as she stepped up to the bed and saw her father's gray skin and sunken eyes. "—been plaguing you again?" she concluded bracingly, in an attempt to cover her consternation.

"So you're here at last, are you? Took you long enough." The voice, which would normally have been a growl, was scarcely more than a whisper.

"We came as soon as we could." Reiterating her words to her brother, she stooped and dropped a kiss onto her father's forehead. "The roads between Exeter and Manchester are quite shocking, you know."

"No more than you should expect, living in such a God-forsaken place," grumbled the duke.

Sir Ethan Brundy, standing behind his wife, could not quite suppress a smile. The duke's contempt for his son-in-law's Lancashire cotton mill had never hindered his willingness to avail himself of its profits.

"Well, don't just stand there!" snapped the duke with a trace of his old manner, struggling to sit up straighter in the bed. "Got something to say to each of you. You first, Helen."

Lady Helen dutifully seated herself on the single straight-backed chair drawn up beside the bed. Sir Ethan gave her shoulder a gentle squeeze, then followed the viscount from the room.

The duke watched them go, but waited until the door closed behind them to remark, "I did all right for you there, didn't I?"

"Where?" asked Lady Helen, feigning ignorance.

"Don't play the wigeon with me! I mean your marriage!" He chuckled with satisfaction at the memory. "Although you were none too happy with my choice at the time."

"No," she conceded. "Nor was I aware that it was you who did the choosing." She was willing to make certain concessions to ease her father's passing, but she would not allow him to take credit for a match that had been all her husband's doing.

"You always were an impertinent chit," he said, not entirely displeased with this show of spirit. "I'll admit, he's not what I would have wanted for you, but I'll not deny he's been good for this family. How old are those boys of yours now?"

"Three," said Lady Helen with a hint of maternal pride at the thought of her twin sons, left to their nurse's care, along with their two younger sisters, while their parents made the hasty trip to Devon.

"I've a small property in Kent that came to me as part of your mother's dowry. I'm leaving it to your elder boy."

"Thank you," Lady Helen said, much moved. "That's very—"

"That way one of 'em won't smell of the shop, at least," continued the duke, considerably cooling his daughter's warmer feelings.

No mention was made of any bequest to his grace's other three grandchildren; nor did Lady Helen expect it. Theirs was a world of male primogeniture, where the eldest son (or, in this case, grandson) took all, and Master William Brundy had the misfortune of being twelve minutes younger than his brother Charles. As for the two girls, the duke had no opinion of females, and gave his granddaughters no more thought than he had given their mother, whose dowry of a paltry five thousand pounds had constituted the fulfilment of his paternal obligation.

"Most of the jewelry will stay here for Tisdale to give his wife someday," rasped the duke, as if in confirmation of this assessment, "but your mother left a pearl ring. Trumpery thing, I daresay, next to the sort of baubles your husband buys you, but it did belong to your mother. It's yours, if you'd like to have it."

"I would, Papa. Thank you."

"One other thing: you're not to go draping yourself in black when I'm gone. Damned waste of money, in my opinion, although I don't doubt your husband could stand the nonsense."

"Yes, he could," said Lady Helen, not without satisfaction.

"Well, he won't, at least not on my account. He'd do better to put his brass into setting that property to rights for that boy of his, as he'll soon find out. Now, if you'll send him in, I've got a thing or two to say to him. No, you may not stay and listen," he added, anticipating her intention of supporting Sir Ethan through the ordeal that awaited him. "Daresay he'll tell you anything he wants you to know."

Lady Helen, who in twenty-five years had learned to pick her battles where her father was concerned, offered no objection, but left the room and joined her husband and brother, who were in hushed consultation with the doctor.

"Ethan, Papa wants a word with you," she said.

Sir Ethan, no doubt expecting a request for money, excused himself to Dr. Grant and returned to his father-in-law.

The duke's relationship with his low-born son-in-law was complicated, although Sir Ethan Brundy, who took people very much as he found them, would have been surprised to hear it described so. To be sure, his grace had never expected to give his daughter to a man such as the one who now stood before him. To the extent that he had considered her future at all, he had thought to see her wed to a gentleman of her own class, preferably one with a title and certainly one who was capable of—and agreeable to—settling a great deal of money on her in order to procure her hand. Sadly, no such gentleman had materialized, and by the time Mr. Ethan Brundy, once an illegitimate workhouse orphan and now the extremely wealthy owner of a cotton mill, had appeared on the scene, the state of his grace's finances had reached such a point that the duke—and, by extension, his daughter—could no longer afford to be choosy.

In the four years since the marriage had taken place, the duke had been pleased to see that his son-in-law was always willing to fund improvements to the home farm or the tenants' cottages, or to advise him of sound investment opportunities on 'Change (although, had his grace but known it, these last were offered so tactfully that the duke was left happy in the erroneous belief that they had been all his own idea), but he still deplored the fellow's obvious vulgarity and unshakeable morality: while the plebeian weaver was more than ready to drop his blunt for causes he considered worthwhile, the duke might coax, wheedle, demand, and rage in vain for funds with which to repay gambling debts. That his son-in-law had recently been knighted for singlehandedly quelling a Luddite riot had altered the duke's opinion not at all; it was just the sort of thing the fellow *would* do.

"Well, what are you standing there gawking at me for?" he demanded, as much as it is possible for a man to make demands in a near-whisper. "Have you never seen a dying man before? Sit down. Got a thing or two to tell you."

Sir Ethan did not bother to defend himself against these unjust charges, but sat down in the chair his wife had recently vacated.

"Grant tells me I'm done for, and although the fellow's a fool, I think he's probably right."

"I'm sorry to 'ear it, your grace."

"Bah!" The duke gave a snort which turned into a cough. Sir Ethan made no attempt to offer assistance, since he knew this would be rebuffed, but waited patiently until his father-in-law regained his breath. "Don't tell me you won't be glad to see the last of a crotchety old bloodsucker, for I won't believe you! Still, I hope you'll oblige me in this. Well, you'll have to, and there's an end on it. Dying man's last request, you know," he added with a rather smug smile.

Sir Ethan shook his head. "If you're thinking to leave me anything, sir, I don't need it."

"*Me*, leave *you* anything? That's a rich one! Mind you, I'm leaving my late wife's dower property to your elder boy, but Helen will tell you about that, or else you'll hear all about it when my will is read. No, my business with you concerns my son."

Sir Ethan was startled into unwise speech. "Tisdale?"

"If I've another son, I'm not aware of it," retorted the duke. "Yes, Tisdale! He's very young to be coming into the title. *I* was almost forty when *my* father died."

" 'e's three-and-twenty," Sir Ethan pointed out. "The same age I was when I in'erited the mill."

The duke glared at him. "There's a vast difference in inheriting a cotton mill and inheriting a dukedom."

Sir Ethan bowed his head in acknowledgement. "There you 'ave me, sir."

"Still, you don't want for sense," said his grace in what was, for him, high praise. "You'll keep him from running himself to ground."

"Oh?" Sir Ethan asked cautiously. "Just what are you asking me, your grace?"

"I've named you as executor of my will."

"Me? Begging your pardon, sir, but why not Tisdale?"

"As I said, he's very young. Depend upon it, when there's an inheritance at stake, folks will come crawling out of the woodwork looking for a piece of it. You'll keep the worst of 'em at bay."

Overseeing the dispensation of a large estate at the exact same time as he was preparing to stand for a seat in the House of Commons was far from an ideal situation. Still, when he recalled his own experiences at the age of three-and-twenty— an age at which he'd not always possessed the wisdom to distinguish true friends from those who sought only to take advantage of him and his newfound wealth—Sir Ethan could not but agree. "I'll do me best, your grace."

"I'll have your word on it that you'll give Theodore any assistance he may require," insisted the duke.

"You 'ave it, sir," the weaver replied without hesitation, offering his hand in proof. His grace took it, his frail, fine-boned fingers all but lost in Sir Ethan's coarser but strong ones.

"That's all right, then," the duke pronounced. His voice sounded steadier now; indeed, a fanciful observer might have been led to believe that he had drawn vigor from his son-in-law's grasp. "You can go back to Helen now, and send Tisdale to me."

Lady Helen, observing the crease in her husband's brow as he emerged from her father's room, immediately drew the worst possible conclusion. "Ethan! Papa—is he—?"

" 'e's not dead—leastways, not yet," he assured her. " 'e wants a word with you, Tisdale."

Running a finger beneath a cravat that suddenly felt too tight, the viscount entered his father's room. The duke had been too hard a parent for his children to regard him with affection, but even in his weakened state, the simple statement "Your father wants a word with you" still had the power to make a knot form in the pit of Theodore's stomach.

"Yes, Papa?" he asked, tentatively approaching his father's bedside. "Ethan said you had something to say to me. What is it?"

"That idiot Grant says I'll be cocking up my toes before I'm much older," the duke said. "You'll be stepping into my shoes soon."

"I'm in no hurry, Papa," the young man assured him.

His grace plucked convulsively at the bedsheets. "Ha! What makes you think you have a choice in the matter? You don't, any more than I have. Any more than I did when I inherited the title from your grandfather. You never knew him—he died when you were still in leading strings—devil of a fellow, though."

"So I've always heard."

"You're not much like him," the duke said, his tone making it clear that this was no compliment. "I am. Your sister is, a little. Pity she wasn't a boy, but there it is."

"I—I'll do my best, sir," said Theodore, feeling some response on his part was called for.

"Daresay you won't botch the thing too badly. Had your share of scrapes, but nothing nine out of ten young fools wouldn't have got into."

Theodore was still trying to decide what response, if any, to make to this very tepid praise when his father continued, "You get into any trouble, you go to your brother, d'ye hear? The fellow's as vulgar as be-damned, but he don't want for sense."

"I daresay I shall contrive," said Theodore, nettled by the suggestion that he, who had been reared from the cradle to assume his father's position someday, should need any assistance, least of all from someone of his brother-in-law's background.

"I daresay you will, seeing as how you don't have a choice," the duke said pettishly. "Now, go away, all of you,

16

and send my man to me. No doubt he and Grant between them will expect me to drink that swill Grant calls medicine, but I'm very tired, and I want to sleep."

"Yes, sir." After a brief, awkward pause, he took his father's withered hand and pressed it to his lips. "Goodnight, Papa."

They were the last words Theodore would ever speak to him. In the middle of the night, he was roused from sleep by his father's valet, bearing the news that the old duke had passed away peacefully in his sleep, and that Theodore, Viscount Tisdale was now the Duke of Reddington.

2

'Tis Pity She's a Whore.
JOHN FORD, title of a play

For Theodore, Duke of Reddington, the days that followed seemed to pass in a blur. There were notices to be sent to the newspapers, of course, but before that, letters must be written and mailed to a host of friends and relations, lest they learn of the duke's death by reading of it in the *Times*. Thankfully, his sister was willing to take on the burden of correspondence, as she and her husband would not return to Lancashire until after the funeral. This left Theodore free to devote his time to other tasks: a meeting with his father's— no, *his*, he realized with some dismay—solicitor, who read the duke's will; another with his banker, who brought him up to date on the state of his father's finances; and, most daunting of all, a lengthy conversation with his steward.

"Thank you for your time, my lord, er, your grace," Alfred began when Theodore entered the study, clearly waiting for the new duke to take his seat behind the desk that had once been his father's. As soon as Theodore had done so, Alfred spread a sheaf of papers across the desk. "I hope I may prevail upon you to undertake at least a few of the improvements I have long urged upon your father. The most ambitious of these is the draining of the south field, but as it would no doubt be unwise to begin such a project so late in the year, I daresay that had best wait until spring. In the meantime, I hope you will consider some of the smaller yet more urgent . . ."

By the time Theodore emerged from the study two hours later, his head was spinning with such matters as bushels per acre, grazing rights, and mining claims.

A few days after his father was laid to rest in the family vault, responses to his sister's letters began to arrive, including four from old friends of the late duke who expressed their willingness to sponsor him if and when he chose to take up his seat in the House of Lords—a responsibility which his father had neglected for so long that Theodore had forgotten it would fall to him along with the rest of his inheritance, and one which would cost him (as his correspondents tactfully pointed out) a rather large sum of money to assume.

It also became apparent that the parish church in one of his father's holdings—no, *his* holdings—was at present without a vicar, for various bishops, rectors, and other churchmen had written to recommend their subordinates for the position.

The post also included several letters from tradesmen whom the old duke owed money, and one or two excruciatingly solicitous communications from gentlemen who began with fond recollections of certain gaming ventures they had enjoyed with his father in happier days when that gentleman still lived, and concluded with expressions of certainty that the young duke would not want to be behindhand in honoring the debts of honor incurred by his never-to-be-sufficiently-mourned sire.

Theodore was so overwhelmed by it all that as soon as the last of the out-of-town relatives had departed, he lost no time in throwing his leg over his horse and riding off hell-for-leather to London, stopping in his bachelor lodgings only long enough to dump his bags before setting out for a discreet house in Half Moon Street, where he lost no time in throwing his leg over the voluptuous form of La Fantasia. Alas, even this pleasant exercise did not provide the escape he sought.

"Mmm, this has been a new experience for me," purred the lady, stretching sinuously and pushing tousled ebony locks from her eyes. "I've never shared a bed with a duke before."

"Not you too, Fanny!" Theodore exclaimed in dismay, sitting bolt upright in the bed.

"Poor darling," she cooed, sitting up behind him so that she might massage his shoulders. "Is it all too much? Shall we go to Paris and get away from it all? Or Rome, perhaps?"

"I'm in mourning," he reminded her. "How would it look for me to go junketing about on the Continent before Papa is cold in his grave? Besides," he added, seeing she was unconvinced by this argument, "I haven't the funds for it in any case."

"But your inheritance—"

He shook his head. "Can't be touched, not until the will

is probated."

"But—but how long will *that* take?" she demanded, not at all pleased with this revelation.

"Lord, how should I know? Old Crumpton—Papa's solicitor, you know—says it might take several months."

"*Months?*" La Fantasia shrieked, before remembering to modify her voice to a seductive purr. "Months? Whatever shall we find to do in the meantime?"

The look she cast him from under her lashes left Theodore in no doubt as to her meaning, but he stood up and reached for his breeches. "I'm sorry, Fanny, but I've a hundred things to do. Truth to tell, it's all a bit much." Seeing her pout, he stroked her rouged cheek with the back of one finger. "Thank you, Fanny. For helping me forget about it, at least for a little while."

La Fantasia, not much mollified by this speech, arranged herself more attractively amidst the rumpled bedclothes, and smiled coyly at him. "Best not take too long, darling. The Earl of Iversleigh has been most assiduous in his attentions, you know."

"I don't doubt it. I'm well aware that I'm the most envied man in London."

She preened a little at the compliment. "Still, you'd best have a care. I won't wait forever, you know." She peeped up at him from under her lashes. "Of course, there are ways to be sure of me."

"Anything," Theodore declared ardently, catching up her hand and pressing passionate kisses into her palm. "You have only to name it, Fanny. You know I adore you! What is it you want? Diamonds? Emeralds? Rubies? Only say the word, and they're yours."

"And how, pray, are you to buy them on the pittance that serves as your allowance?"

"It's only for a little while, and it may not take that long, after all. In the meantime, I'm sure my credit is good."

She gave a disdainful sniff. "I thought I might go for a drive in St. James's this afternoon. I wonder if I might see Lord Iversleigh there?"

"Don't toy with me, Fanny! Tell me what it is that you want."

She rose slowly from the bed, and the sheets fell away to reveal the full glory of her figure. "Every duke needs a duchess, you know," she said huskily.

"*M-Marriage?*" Theodore stammered, his ardor considerably cooled. "You want—you expect me to offer you marriage?"

"You said I might have anything I wanted," she reminded him.

"Yes, but—but—dash it, Fanny, I'm not ready to marry anyone just yet!"

"I shan't object to a long engagement," she said reassuringly. "Let us say, just as long as it takes for the will to be probated."

He gave a shaky little laugh, but he had the lowering conviction that she was not joking. "You—you don't understand—"

"Oh, I understand very well!" she cried, her exquisite body flushing a mottled red hue.

"I meant no offense, Fan," he said hastily. "It's just that, well, my position, you know—I have a responsibility —"

"In other words, I'm good enough for a tumble 'twixt the sheets, but your duchess must be a virgin!"

"Not necessarily," Theodore protested. "I might not object to a young widow."

Having clarified this point, he picked up his shirt and pulled it over his head, and thus failed to observe the warning signs of the approaching storm. His head emerged from the neck of his shirt just in time to see his inamorata snatch a china shepherdess from over the mantel.

"Get out!" she screeched in accents more suited to a Billingsgate fishwife than an aspiring duchess, and hurled the ornament at his head.

He ducked only just in time, and the shepherdess shattered against the wall behind him. "Here now, Fan, there's no cause for—"

"Get—*out!*" she shrieked again, and a porcelain vase followed the shepherdess, glancing off Theodore's shoulder as she berated him with a vocabulary he had not known she had possessed, including a few words that were unfamiliar to him in spite of a fairly comprehensive education on the subject at first Eton and then Oxford.

"Fanny, I meant no—I'm sorry—*ow!*—Dash it, Fan, be reasonable—"

But La Fantasia, that most courted of all London courtesans, was in no mood for reason. When a crystal candy dish was hurled in his direction, followed in rapid succession by two brass candlesticks and a small ormolu clock, Theodore decided discretion was indeed the better part of valor. He snatched up the rest of his clothes and beat a hasty retreat, sped on his way by what trinkets La Fantasia could lay her hands on as she chased after him down the stairs and out of the house.

Thus his grace the Duke of Reddington, taking leave of his mistress while hopping on one foot in an attempt to tug on his boot—his collar open, his cravat hanging loosely about his neck, his coat and waistcoat caught up over his arm, and his other boot clutched in one hand, held out before him as if it might offer some protection from the hellish fury of a woman scorned.

At last the door slammed shut behind him, and Theodore, judging it safe, stopped on the pavement long enough to put on his other boot and shrug his arms into his coat and waistcoat. He glanced up and down the street, but took little comfort in the fact that there were no carriages visible in what was primarily a quiet residential street. Word of the fracas would certainly get out; these things always did, conveyed from the servants of one house to the servants of another and thence from servants to masters, until everyone from the lowliest scullery maid to the Marquess of Cutliffe himself, who occupied a house on the other end of the street when he was in Town, would have got wind of it. From there, of course, word would spread to other houses in other streets via the gentlemen's clubs and the ladies' tea parties, until all of London would know of it.

In truth, though, Theodore's sense of humiliation sprang from other causes than his being the target of La Fantasia's rage. He had known, of course, that she had accepted him as her protector solely on his expectations; why else would she have chosen a green fellow almost a decade her junior over the more mature and, yes, more sophisticated charms of men like Iversleigh? He had known exactly where his attraction lay, and it had troubled him not at all; in fact, he had considered it one of the advantages of being the heir to a dukedom. But to think that she had taken him on in the belief that he was gullible enough to be cozened into marriage? The insult was more than flesh and blood could bear. The dull ache in his shoulder where one of her missiles had found its mark was nothing to the blow to his self-esteem.

Still, he had not been on the Town this long without learning to a nicety how the game should be played. When a man broke off with his mistress (and one might certainly argue that it had certainly been *he* who had broken off with *her*, by refusing to acquiesce to her last and most outrageous request), he gave the woman her *congé* in the form of an expensive farewell gift. Well, La Fantasia would soon discover that her erstwhile protector was no less a knowing one than any gentleman many years his senior. He stopped by his flat only long enough to put on fresh clothing (including a black band on the sleeve of his coat to indicate his bereaved state), then set out for Rundell and Bridge, jewelers to the king for longer than Theodore had been alive.

He had not exaggerated when he'd told La Fantasia that his credit was good. Mssrs. Philip Rundell and John Bridge had not attained their present position without keeping *au courant* with the doings of the aristocracy, and they were quick to offer their condolences to the young man who entered their establishment with his jaw set, yet something of vulnerability in his green eyes.

"And what may we show you today, your grace?" Mr. Rundell asked at the conclusion of these expressions of sympathy. "Dare we hope there is soon to be a new Duchess of Reddington? It has been a long time, I believe, since that title was graced by your late mother. I had the honor of designing her wedding ring."

Theodore, ignoring these hints, came straight to the point. "Show me the most expensive thing you've got."

This, when it was brought out from the back room and the safe in which it usually resided, proved to be an ornate necklace so laden with diamonds, rubies, emeralds, and sapphires that it might have served any knight of old as a breastplate. In truth, Theodore found it more than a little vulgar. In spite of his bleak mood, a smile tugged at his lips at the thought of his brother-in-law presenting so gaudy a piece to his sister—as he might well have done in the early days of their marriage, before she had taken on the task of informing her husband's tastes. But its vulgarity, Theodore decided, was perfectly in keeping with the woman upon whom he intended to bestow it, the same woman from whose presence he had been driven only a few hours earlier.

"I'll take it," he pronounced.

His resolution suffered a slight check when he was informed of the price of this token, but the ache in his shoulder served to strengthen his resolve. He would send the piece to La Fantasia, and be vindicated when the *ton* whispered behind its hands that Tisdale—no, Reddington!—had behaved just as he ought. As for the gift's recipient, let her own actions bear witness to her unsuitability for the position she coveted; his own conduct would be above reproach.

"Excellent, excellent!" exclaimed Mr. Rundell, who had secretly feared that the showy piece of his partner's design was a bit *much*, and that they would eventually be obliged to remove the gemstones and melt down the gold in order to fashion less ambitious, yet more marketable, examples of the jeweler's art.

"Er, I haven't the funds to pay for it today," Theodore began, only to be cut short.

"No need to trouble yourself, my lord—er, your grace," Mr. Rundell assured him hastily. "I'm sure we can repose every confidence in you to settle your account after your affairs have been set in order. Now, shall you present it to the lady yourself, or would you prefer to have it delivered?"

Theodore considered with some satisfaction the vision of himself bestowing the necklace upon La Fantasia in person, nobly forgiving her for her ill treatment of him even as he gently but firmly rebuffed her tearful pleas for him to take her back. Gratifying as this vision was, he was practical enough to acknowledge that she was more likely to throw something at his head than to beg for a reconciliation; La Fantasia, he knew from experience, was not the begging kind.

"Deliver it to Half Moon Street," he said decisively. "Number nineteen." He requested paper and pen with which he might compose a note, and upon this being brought, he scrawled, *Let this token serve to express my best wishes for your future happiness. It has been a most educational experience.* La Fantasia, he felt sure, would recognize the double meaning. Out of long habit, he signed himself simply *T* for Tisdale, then, after a moment's consideration, added several letters and a few words, so that it read *Theodore, Duke of Reddington.*

3

How well those live who are comfortably and thoroughly
in debt . . . how jolly and easy they are in their minds.
WILLIAM MAKEPEACE THACKERAY, *Vanity Fair*

Having dispatched La Fantasia to, presumably, the eager arms of Lord Iversleigh, Theodore found himself sadly at loose ends. London was extremely thin of company in autumn, and would very likely remain so until Parliament reconvened in November. And even if the *ton* had been in residence and the Season in full spate, the fact that he was in mourning would have precluded his participation in most of its diversions. The thought of spending the night alone in his bachelor flat was intolerable: Besides dwelling on his quarrel with La Fantasia and how he might have handled the matter differently, he was all too aware that he must give up the flat soon and take up residence in the town house that had been his father's and *his* father's before him. Having nothing else to do and nowhere else to go, he eventually ended up at White's, where the Dukes of Reddington had been members since its earliest days as a chocolate house more than a century ago. His father, he recalled, had put him up for membership upon his leaving Oxford, and his unanimous acceptance into the exclusive club was one of the few occasions on which he'd had the satisfaction of knowing he had made the duke proud. Granted, the play in its card rooms tended to run a bit deep, and his pockets were to let, at least until the will was probated. Still, as he had told Fanny, his credit was good. Besides, he thought in a burst of optimism, he might even win.

He had not expected to find the club crowded, and nor was it; still, there were several gentlemen present who were old acquaintances of either himself or his father. Chief among the former were four young men very nearly his own age. They had all been at Oxford together, and all were heirs to titles of varying degrees of preeminence. With the callousness of youth, they had dubbed themselves the Lads-in-Waiting, and had sworn an oath (with much pricking of fingers and mixing of blood, which had lent the business just that degree of solemnity and high drama sure to appeal to very young men of seventeen) that each one, upon succeeding to his father's honors, would treat the others to a toast with the club's best brandy. Three of the group had already made good on this promise, so Theodore, not wishing to appear behindhand in the matter, was quick to follow the precedent that had been set for him. The famed bow window overlooking St. James's Street was vacant upon this occasion, since Lord Alvanley and his set were absent from Town—Alvanley being, of course, the acknowledged leader of fashionable Society since Brummell had decamped for France four years earlier—and so the three young lords seized the opportunity of ensconcing themselves there. From this lofty position, they offered Theodore their condolences upon his father's death, adding (in the same breath and without a hint of irony) their congratulations upon his coming into the title, along with caveats that the responsibilities of such a position posed a serious impediment to such pleasures as they had envisioned during their Oxford days. As this information merely confirmed the discovery that Theodore had come to London to escape, he was not sorry when one of the group (the only one whose father still lived, and thus the only one who could contribute nothing to the conversation) suggested they pop into the card room for a look.

Here they found a game of whist in progress, and when one of the participants was obliged to take his leave, Theodore did not have to be persuaded to take his place at the card table. Alas, it soon proved he was no luckier at cards that evening than he had been at love earlier in the day. He soon found himself punting on tick, but as the only alternative was to return to that lonely flat, he was easily coaxed into playing one more hand, and then another, and another. His losses did not trouble him overmuch; after all, this was nothing like that occasion some four years earlier, when he had been duped into playing hazard with a villain who only wanted some hold over his sister. For one thing, this was cards, not dice, and the game was as much one of skill as it was of chance. For another, he was not dependent upon his wealthy brother-in-law for the money to cover his losses, but would have the funds himself as soon as the duke's will was probated. Until then, his credit was good.

Still, when the game broke up he was a bit taken aback by the sum he'd managed to lose in a very short space of time. He stammered something about seeing his banker in the morning, after which he would do himself the honor of calling upon his opponent for the purpose of redeeming his vowels.

"No trouble at all, your grace," the other man quickly demurred, and upon this reassuring note, Theodore took his leave.

* * *

Alas, the following morning it became abundantly clear to Theodore that there was one place in London where his credit was, in fact, *not* good. It was his misfortune that this place happened to be the Bank of England.

"But dash it, man!" he expostulated with the stoop-shouldered clerk on the other side of a metal grill that gave him the appearance of a mouse in a cage. "You know who I am! You've seen me a hundred times!"

"Yes, your lordship—that is, your grace—and I'm sorry I can't oblige you, but there are rules—"

"Never mind the rules! Is old Dorry in? I'll have a word with him, if you please."

The clerk, caught between offending a very influential client and angering his superior—for the personage whom Theodore had so cavalierly dubbed "Old Dorry" was, in fact, Mr. George Dorrien, Governor of the Bank of England—wavered only a moment before coming to a decision.

"Yes, sir—er, your grace—yes, Mr. Dorrien is here. I'll fetch him directly, shall I?"

As it was he who had suggested it, Theodore raised no

objections to this plan. The hapless clerk escaped from his cage and hurried across the marble-tiled floor, disappearing through a door in the rear where, presumably, the bank's senior officers might be found. He returned a few minutes later, trotting along at the heels of a tall man whose stern visage melted into smiles at the sight of his noble client.

"Well, well, I see we must accustom ourselves to calling you 'your grace' now," he said, taking the hand Theodore offered and pumping it vigorously. "I was sorry to read in the *Times* of your father's passing. Still, I have no doubt you will fill his shoes admirably. Now, how may I be of service to you?"

Theodore told him, and the ingratiating smile faded.

"Dear me, your grace," he said fretfully, "I wish I could oblige you, but I'm afraid I can't."

"Dash it, Dorry, you knew my father," Theodore reminded him. "You've seen me come in here with him since I was in leading strings!" This was an exaggeration, for the duke had never taken the slightest interest in babes in arms, even when the babes were his own. Still, the banker readily conceded the point.

"I have indeed, and you may be sure we have always valued the patronage of the Dukes of Reddington. You know, I daresay, that one of your ancestors signed the bank's original charter. For that reason alone, I wish I could provide you with the advance you seek. Unfortunately, there are laws about these things—the shareholders, you know—"

Alas, none of Theodore's arguments—and he put forth many—could move the bank's governor from this stance.

Eventually he was forced to take his leave, feeling very much like a dog with its tail tucked between its legs. He returned to his flat, where his valet greeted him with the unwelcome news that the early post had been delivered—unwelcome because among the letters that had been forwarded to him from his father's—no, *his*—estate in Devon were several requests for payment from various tradesmen in both London and Exeter. When Theodore cast these aside and picked up the *Times*, he discovered the reason for the inundation: there amongst the advertisements was a notice inviting all to whom the late Duke of Reddington had owed remuneration to submit their requests in writing within the next ninety days. It was signed, "Sir Ethan Brundy, executor."

"Are you trying to bankrupt me before I even get my hands on the money?" Theodore grumbled under his breath. "Dash it, Ethan!"

Ethan . . . at the sight of the name printed in bold black type, a new plan began to take form in Theodore's brain. Ethan, his sister's husband and his own brother by marriage, who had towed his father out of the River Tick more than once during the past four years, and who was now executor of the duke's will . . . Ethan, who was standing for Parliament, and who would be returning to London very soon for just that purpose . . .

Theodore discovered he could now face the more pressing of his obligations in a state resembling equilibrium. He left his flat and betook himself to the Reddington town house, where he made arrangements for taking up residence, the foremost of these being to send for the butler, the cook, and certain other servants from the country estate. Even the pile of bills that awaited him on a small table in the foyer had no more power to trouble him, for he had formed a plan, and as soon as his brother-in-law returned to his own town house in nearby Grosvenor Square, he would put this plan into action.

That night he enjoyed no better luck at White's than he had the night before. Still, he slept soundly for the first time since the night his father died, convinced that his troubles would soon be at an end.

* * *

His sister, by contrast, was not of so sanguine a frame of mind. Seated with her husband at the breakfast table of their home in Lancashire, Lady Helen frowned thoughtfully at the letter in her hand.

"Bad news, love?" asked Sir Ethan, who had looked up from his newspaper to make some remark to his wife and noted her puckered brow.

"I don't know," she confessed without looking up from her reading. "To be sure, some of it is very good news indeed. And yet—darling, when you reach London, will you oblige me by looking in on Teddy?"

"Aye, but I'd 'ave done so in any case. What's troubling you?"

In answer, she handed him the single sheet of foolscap bearing the wax seal (now broken) of the Marquess of Cutliffe. "It seems he and that dreadful female they call La Fantasia are quite exploded."

"I'd 'ave thought you'd be glad of that," he remarked as

he scanned the letter.

"Yes, but it appears there's more. Evidently their break was quite—quite *public*, and since then the woman has been seen at the theatre sporting a shockingly vulgar necklace which she claims was a parting gift from the Duke of Reddington. Meanwhile, rumor has it that Teddy has been dipping rather deep at White's. Ethan, you don't suppose he's reached *point non plus* already, do you?"

"Don't fret yourself, love. When a single young man in'erits a dukedom, 'e's bound to be the object of a certain amount of interest. I doubt it's as serious as all that."

"Yes, but this comes from Emily—Lady Cutliffe, you know," she insisted. "It's not just idle gossip."

"I didn't know there was any other kind," he remarked, setting down his coffee cup and pushing back his chair.

"If you ask me," said Lady Helen with some asperity, "what Teddy needs is a woman!"

"I thought 'e 'ad one," pointed out her spouse. "In fact, I thought that was 'alf the trouble."

She gave him a reproachful look. "I don't mean that dreadful creature he's had in keeping for the past two months—'La Fantasia,' indeed! No, I mean Teddy needs a wife. Not a schoolroom miss, mind you, but a sensible woman his own age. When I join you in London, I might introduce him to one or two likely candidates who might serve the purpose. It is a pity that our being in mourning will put a damper on our engagements—no dancing, certainly, even if there are any balls being hosted so late in the year, which I doubt—but we might make up a theatre party, and your

Parliamentary bid might offer a few opportunities, as we will be obliged to host a few dinner parties." As her husband failed to second this suggestion, she was obliged to solicit his opinion. "Well? What do you think?"

"I think 'e's already got one big sister. 'e won't be needing another."

"Surely you cannot deny that marriage to the right woman might go a long way toward settling him down!"

"Oh, I'll not deny that. But I never 'eard of any young man accustomed to a game pullet like La Fantasia suddenly brought to 'eel by a sensible female 'oo's practically on the shelf."

"All right, then," retorted Lady Helen, stung, "what sort of woman do *you* think would suit him?"

He considered the question for a long moment before answering. "One 'oo'll make 'im want to be a man."

She gave a little huff of derision. "I thought that's what women like La Fantasia were for."

"I don't doubt she makes 'im *feel* like one," he said, laying aside his serviette and rising from the table. " 'eaven knows she ought to, if 'e's paying 'er even a fraction of what rumor claims she charges. But I'm talking about a girl 'oo'll make 'im want to *be* one—the less pleasant parts included."

"Oh?" she asked coyly, giving him her hand and allowing him to pull her to her feet. "And what parts might those be?"

"Tending to responsibilities when 'e'd rather concentrate on pleasures, for one thing. I wish you were going with me, love," he added in a wistful tone.

"So do I," she answered in the same vein. "But we agreed that it would be unwise to take William out until his sore throat is rather better."

"And I know 'ow much you were looking forward to entertaining a bunch of Whig leaders' wives to tea," he retorted playfully.

"Deprived of my life's ambition," she agreed, shaking her head mournfully. "I promise, as soon as William is able to travel, I shall join you in London and play the political hostess as enthusiastically as you could wish."

As his wife came from a long line of Tories, Sir Ethan recognized this as no small sacrifice, and expressed his appreciation so thoroughly that he was still in the act when the footman came to begin clearing the table. Releasing her with a sigh, Sir Ethan nevertheless kept his arm about her waist as she accompanied him to the front door, where the carriage awaited that would convey him to London and the launching of his Parliamentary bid.

"Never mind about your brother, love. I'll see if I can discover what's toward."

With this promise, he kissed her again, expressed his hope that Willie's recovery would not be long delayed, then climbed into the carriage and settled himself comfortably against the squabs.

"All right, Theodore," he muttered aloud as the horses were whipped up and the vehicle started forward, "let's see what devilry you've got up to this time."

4

Submit to the present evil, lest a greater one befall you.
PHAEDRUS, *Fables*

"Hallo, Ethan!" exclaimed Theodore, rising from his chair as Sir Ethan Brundy was shown into the drawing room of his flat by his valet, the butler and the other servants having not yet arrived from Reddington Hall. "Deuced cold outside— come have a seat before the fire. Will you have a drop to take the chill off? There's brandy in the decanter, but if you'd rather have something else—I don't know exactly what Papa had laid down in his cellars, but I daresay we can find out. As they say, there's no time like the present."

Sir Ethan assured him that brandy would suit him very well, then sank into the nearest of two overstuffed armchairs and accepted the pot-bellied glass of brandy from his brother-in-law's hand.

"Did you only arrive in Town today, then?" Theodore continued. "But where's Nell? Does she not accompany you?"

If Sir Ethan had not already had reason to suspect

39

something was amiss with the young duke, Theodore's sudden loquaciousness would have been enough to inform him of it. "No, she'll be coming later. Willie's taken ill."

"Poor little fellow." Theodore grinned suddenly. "Or should I say 'poor Nell'? Daresay Willie out of sorts is enough to overset the whole household."

Sir Ethan swirled the liquid in his glass, then helped himself to a sip. "Now you know what really brings me to London," he confided with an impish smile. It was not true, of course, but it struck just the right note to induce Theodore to exchange confidences with him.

"I should think so! Willie in a temper is enough to make any man turn tail and run." In a carefully offhand manner that did not deceive his brother-in-law for a moment, he added, "Truth to tell, Ethan, I'm deuced glad you're here. I'd be obliged to you if you can advance me something on my inheritance—just enough to tide me over until the will is probated, you know."

Sir Ethan shook his head. "Much as I'd like to oblige you, I can't."

"You *can't?* But—well, but dash it, Ethan! You're the executor, aren't you?"

"Aye, I am."

"Well, then—"

"Theodore, all that means is that I'm charged with making sure the terms of your father's will are carried out the way 'e intended—and that includes seeing to it that everything is done open and aboveboard."

"But it's my own money, dash it!" Theodore protested.

Sir Ethan nodded. "Aye, and you'll get it, all in good time."

"Good time for *you*, maybe!"

"Aye, and for you. After all, you'd not like it if I started doling out legacies to your father's valet, or housekeeper, or butler, would you?"

"No, but—"

"But the money's rightfully theirs," he added with a look of bland innocence in his brown eyes. "It says so in the will."

"It's not at all the same thing!"

"It is so far as the law is concerned. If I were to distribute so much as a farthing from your father's estate before probate is granted, I'd open meself up to legal action." In an attempt to ease the young man's obvious distress, he added in a lighter tone, "A pretty fellow I'd look, standing for Parliament with that 'anging over me 'ead! I might as well 'and the election to Sir Valerian Wadsworth on a silver platter."

Theodore, however, was not to be distracted. "But I would be the logical one to bring any such action against you, and it's not like I'm going to prefer charges against you for giving my money to *me!*"

"*You* might not do so, but your father's lawyer might," his brother pointed out. " 'e'd be within 'is rights, too. In fact, 'e might even consider it an obligation to 'is grace."

"Crumpton is *my* lawyer now—and he'd do well to remember it!"

"Aye, that 'e is. And if you know 'e can't be trusted to look out for your father's interests, 'ow can you trust 'im to look after yours?" Seeing that this observation had

41

momentarily deprived his young relation of speech, Sir Ethan added gently, "What's the matter, you young fool? Surely you 'aven't got yourself rolled up within a se'ennight of in'eriting the title?"

"I'm not 'rolled up,' " Theodore protested. "I've got plenty of money—or I will have, as soon as it comes into my possession."

"Is it that little ladybird you've 'ad in keeping?"

"No—that is, not entirely, but—dash it, Ethan, she expected me to marry her! I may have been green, but I'm not such a flat as all *that!* And when she saw I couldn't be persuaded, or seduced, or coerced into it—" He broke off, shuddering at the memory.

"Didn't take it well, did she?" Sir Ethan observed knowingly.

Theodore gave him a rather sheepish grin. "Lord, you never saw such a shrew! It made me think that perhaps I'm well out of a bad business—Iversleigh may have her with my blessing! But I couldn't let it get about that *she'd* ditched *me,* so I went to Rundell and Bridge and bought her the most expensive thing they had."

Sir Ethan, who had bestowed upon his wife more than one bauble from this establishment and thus had a very good idea of the prices to be found therein, gave a long, low whistle.

"And then," Theodore continued, "I went to White's and—well, I just wanted to forget about it, just for a little while—not just Fanny, mind you, but all of it: the dukedom, and the steward and his blasted 'improvements,' and the House of Lords, where I'll no doubt be expected to take my seat, and—oh, you don't understand!"

"Actually, I do," said his brother with a faraway look in his eyes. "More than you think."

Theodore, intent on his own troubles, paid no heed to the interruption. "And I can't let it get out that the Duke of Reddington don't pay his debts, for we've had quite enough of that in the family already! But I don't have to tell *you* that— God knows you shelled out enough blunt, towing Papa out of the River Tick." At this recollection, a new possibility occurred to him. "I say, Ethan, I don't suppose you would be willing to lend me the ready? Just until the will is probated, you know, and at any interest rate you care to name," he added hastily, lest his brother-in-law balk at agreeing to this proposal.

Sir Ethan gave him an appraising look, and asked, " 'ow much do you need?"

Theodore told him.

"You've managed to run through that much in less than a fortnight?" demanded his brother-in-law, staring at him.

"No!" Theodore said, bristling. "That is, I'll admit I've spent more than I should, but old Crumpton says the will could take months! A fellow has to have something to live on in the meantime, you know."

"Never mind that! 'ow much will it take to settle your gaming debts and pay for the trinket you gave that game pullet?"

This figure, while still much higher than it ought to have been, seemed quite reasonable compared to the sum Theodore had felt necessary to sustain him for the few months it might take for the will to go through probate.

"All right, then," pronounced Sir Ethan. "It's yours."

Theodore was moved to seize his brother's hand and wring it gratefully. "I say, Ethan, you're a great gun! You'll have every penny of it back, I promise—and, as I said, at any rate of interest you care to name."

Sir Ethan shook his head. "There'll be no interest. As for paying me back, you don't 'ave to do that—at least, not in pounds, shillings, and pence."

This assurance left Theodore more than a little puzzled. "What do you want, then? Does it have to do with your Parliamentary bid? I'll be glad to use any influence I may have—"

Sir Ethan had to smile at this sincere but misguided offer. "I'm not sure but what the influence of a Tory might do me more 'arm than good."

"I daresay it might," Theodore acknowledged with a grin. "What, then—?"

"You'll pay me back by working it off." In case further explanation was needed, he added, "In the mill."

Theodore's grin faded, replaced by an expression that combined bewilderment with indignation. "Me? Work in a cotton mill? You can't be serious!"

"Perfectly serious," Sir Ethan assured him, and although his tone was pleasant enough, there was something in his eyes that gave Theodore pause.

"Dash it, Ethan, I won't do it!"

"I guess you'll 'ave to wait until the will is probated, then," Sir Ethan said sympathetically, and rose to take his leave.

"No, but—but dash it, Ethan!" Theodore expostulated. "You can't—you really *can't* expect me to work in a cotton mill!"

"Why not? Men do it every day," pointed out Sir Ethan.

"But—but I'm the Duke of Reddington! How would it look for me to—to—?"

"No one need know 'oo you are unless you choose to tell 'em," his brother assured him. "I can promise you that I won't. In any case, it won't be for long—only until probate is granted."

"But old Crumpton says that could take months!"

"Most of the mill workers will work their entire lives and never see such a sum," said Sir Ethan, hardening his heart.

"I'll tell my sister about this!" Theodore cried hotly. "Nell won't stand for it!"

"When I left 'elen," Sir Ethan recalled blandly, "she 'ad the fixed intention of introducing you to one or two females— not schoolroom misses, mind you, but sensible females 'oo might inspire you to settle down."

"Oh, God!" groaned Theodore, clutching his golden locks in dismay.

"Come, Theodore, what 'ave you got to lose? It's not as if there are that many entertainments to be found in Town this time of year, anyway. Besides, I thought you young bucks were up to any kind of lark. I'll wager it would be something none of your cronies have done."

"No, but everyone will think I've slunk back to Devon to nurse a broken heart for La Fantasia."

"Not if you put it about that you've been obliged to leave Town and look into your estate. Your papa left several, and you need not say which one it is that demands your attention."

"And what if something really *does* demand my attention?"

"You can give instructions that any letters are to be forwarded to me. No one will wonder at it, since I'm the executor of your father's will, and I'll know where to find you."

Theodore gave a short laugh that was utterly devoid of humor. "You seem to have it all worked out, never mind the fact that I'll stand out like a mustard pot in a coal scuttle."

"Aye, you will if you dress like that," Sir Ethan agreed, casting a critical eye over his young relation's fashionable tailcoat of Bath superfine, buckskin breeches, and gleaming Hessian boots. "You'll want some more suitable clothes."

"I suppose I'll just order them from Weston," retorted Theodore.

"You might. Or you could 'ave your man buy you some things from the secondhand shops in Petticoat Lane."

"And how, pray, am I to explain my sudden taste for castoff clothing?"

Sir Ethan gave Theodore the same sweet, disarming smile that had—eventually—won his sister's fickle heart. "Can you wonder at it? Just tell 'im you lost a wager."

"*Touché*," Theodore acknowledged with a grin. "Now that you mention it, that would serve as an excuse for anyone who might wonder why I'm working at the mill, yet putting up at its owner's house."

Sir Ethan shook his head. "I'm sorry, Theodore, but I'm afraid that won't do. No one at the mill is to know 'oo you are, for I won't 'ave them giving you special treatment."

"I suppose they would be bound to do so, if they knew I was a duke," Theodore conceded generously.

"They would be bound to do so if they knew you were a relation of mine," Sir Ethan corrected him gently. "But there's a boarding'ouse not far from the mill, kept by a gentlewoman 'oo's fallen on 'ard times. Not only would it give you a roof over your 'ead, but you'd 'ave someone to cook your dinner and do your washing. You'd also be doing a kindness for an unfortunate lady and 'er daughter."

Theodore, listening to these plans for his future with a sense of fatal resignation, made no reply. At the moment, he could imagine no one more unfortunate than himself.

5

A simple maiden in her flower
Is worth a hundred coats-of-arms.
ALFRED, LORD TENNYSON, *Lady Clara Vere de Vere*

Daphne Drinkard emerged from the back of the house with an armful of freshly laundered sheets destined for the second-best bedroom. This chamber, which had once been her own, was usually vacant these days, kept in readiness for anyone willing to pay half a crown per night for its use, while Daphne occupied a much smaller room at the opposite end of the hall. Not, she reminded herself, that she resented this; in fact, she much preferred it to her mama's protestations that mother and daughter should share the bedroom which had once belonged to the late Mr. Drinkard. But Daphne, who had already lost so much in the three years since that gentleman's death, had been determined not to add her privacy to that constantly growing list. Suppressing a sigh at the memory of the cheerful room with its flowered chintz curtains and thick Axminster carpet, she went in search of her mother to inform her that the laundry maid (who, along with the cook, represented all that remained of what had once been a sizeable staff) had said they were almost out of fuller's earth.

She found Mrs. Drinkard in the front hall, deep in conversation with a man Daphne had never seen before. That the conversation was causing her mother considerable perturbation of spirits was quite clear, for her mother's lace-mittened hands gestured in agitation.

"But here is my daughter now! Daphne, my love, come and make your curtsy to Sir Valerian Wadsworth."

Thus adjured, Daphne dipped a curtsy, clutching the bedsheets against her chest lest they tip over and tumble onto the floor, undoing the laundry maid's work as well as her own, since it was she to whom fell the task of folding.

"How do you do, sir?" she responded politely.

"The better for having made your acquaintance, Miss Drinkard, I'm sure," he said, his smile exposing a mouthful of impossibly white teeth.

"Will you be staying with us, then?" She made a quick appraisal of his fashionable attire and stylishly disheveled chestnut locks, and determined that here was one who could well afford the second-best bedroom. Color rose to her face at the thought of this gentleman sleeping in the bed that had once been hers.

"Dear me, no," her mother put in hastily. "Sir Valerian is putting up at one of the fashionable hotels in Manchester."

"As I was telling your mother, I wish to hold a series of meetings—for the mill workers, you understand—and wondered if she might have a public room I could hire for the purpose."

"Sir Valerian is standing for Parliament," put in Mrs. Drinkard by way of explanation. "Only fancy! I told him he might use the dining room, once dinner has been served and the dishes cleared away."

Daphne had to admire her mother's adroitness in leaving the impression, without going so far as to lie about it, that these menial tasks would fall to persons other than themselves. Sir Valerian said all that was proper and took his leave, promising to see them again on the following night, when he would hold the first of his meetings.

The door had no sooner closed behind him than her mother fell into raptures. "Oh, my dear! A baronet! Perhaps even a Member of Parliament! If only he should take a fancy to you, we could all be comfortable again! It would be just the sort of match you might have made if your dear papa had not died! You would be Lady Wadsworth, you know, and have a grand house in London where you should live during the Season, and whenever Parliament was in session—"

"Mama, pray hold your transports!" Daphne protested, laughing. "The man has only just laid eyes on me—never mind the fact that he has not yet secured his seat in the Commons."

"I'm sure he could not fail to do so—such an air! Such address! Yes, I know you think I am very silly," she chided her irreverent daughter, "but you cannot know how I have feared for your future, my dearest girl."

In fact, Daphne had a very good idea, for she often experienced those same fears herself. Three years ago, she had been seventeen years old, and preparing to go to London for her first Season, where she had every expectation of making a good match. Her birth, though not aristocratic, was certainly genteel, and her dowry was respectable. As for her physical attributes, she was much admired in Lancashire, and it was unlikely that gentlemen in London would be less appreciative of glossy brown curls, speaking brown eyes, and a trim figure than were their Lancastrian counterparts. She was intelligent, without being a bluestocking; in fact, she was a poetess of some note, having even known the satisfaction of seeing several of these pieces published in various journals, from which she had even received a modest payment. Alas, now that she and her mother could have used the extra money, this source of income was closed to her: the poetry in which she had once taken such pleasure had taken a dark turn of late, usually addressing such subjects as the cruelty of fate and the blighting of youthful hopes. Unlike their sunnier pre-decessors, these had never seen print; in fact, they were no sooner penned than they were consigned to the fire. Quite aside from the fact that no publisher would release upon an unsuspecting public such works as must cast their readers into a fit of the dismals, Daphne had no desire for them to bring pain to her mother.

For with the death of Mr. Drinkard, a tragedy of another sort (albeit not unrelated to the first) had come upon the household. No sooner had he been laid to rest than it was brought home to mother and daughter that their situation was dire indeed. The sweet-tempered and somewhat bookish gentleman they had known as husband and father had proven to be nothing more than a façade behind which had hidden a very different man, one whose frequent trips on unnamed "estate business" had, in fact, been sojourns to Newmarket, Royal Ascot, and several lesser temples to horseracing, as well as shorter jaunts to numerous cockpits and prizefights. Mr. Drinkard was, in short, a hardened gambler. This might have been forgiven had he been even moderately successful at this dubious pastime, but he was not. He was an indifferent judge of horseflesh and a worse one of men, staking his ever-shrinking capital on the favorites of his younger days in blithe disregard for the fact that these former pets of the Fancy were now past their prime. Daphne's dowry was long gone, and most of the assets that had remained to the widow and child of the deceased had been sold to pay his debts. Only the house remained, its conversion to a boarding house (demeaning though it was) being the only thing that had kept it, too, from the auction block.

As for Daphne's approaching Season, it had never been spoken of again. It would have been impossible to have gone to London in any case, as she and her mother were now in mourning, and by the time they had put off their blacks, it had been made abundantly plain to that young lady, by now eighteen, that there was no money for such an endeavor, and it was unlikely that there ever would be. Orders for ball gowns, riding habits, and opera cloaks had been abruptly canceled, and most of the dresses that had already been delivered from the modiste had been stripped of their ribbons and lace, and the denuded garments dyed black. Only a few had escaped the vat: the two day dresses which she alternated wearing on weekdays (now three years old and beginning to show wear at seams and elbows); one walking dress which she wore to church on Sundays; a simple dinner gown which, according to Mrs. Drinkard, gave the boarding house an air of gentility when Daphne wore it downstairs for the evening meal; and a pink satin ball gown, never worn, still wrapped in its original tissue and tucked away in the attic where— unbeknownst to her mother—Daphne slipped away to visit it occasionally, furtively fanning the tiny ember of hope that, in the teeth of all evidence, refused to be utterly extinguished.

Yes, Daphne had every reason to fear for her future, which seemed to promise nothing but a life of spinsterhood and near-poverty. The husband she was to have found in London was destined to remain undiscovered (and might well have married another by this time, in any case), and her Lancashire beaux had all melted away as soon as her changed circumstances had become public knowledge.

Her mother's thoughts must have been running along very similar lines, for Mrs. Drinkard said, in a voice half doubt and half hope, "I don't suppose you might wear the pink satin tomorrow night?"

"A ball gown? Mama, you must know better! I might as well throw myself at the poor man's head!"

"I only thought he might notice you," Daphne's parent said defensively.

"He would certainly do that, for he would think me the most shockingly vulgar creature imaginable!"

Mrs. Drinkard heaved a sigh of regret. "I suppose you're right. Tell me, do you think we should set out a bottle of your poor papa's brandy? I suppose not—we wouldn't want to waste it on the mill workers. Why does he want to meet with them, do you suppose?"

Daphne offered no opinion, for at that moment the door opened and a new arrival stood on the threshold, the autumn sun striking his bare head and turning his fair hair to gold. He was quite tall, and although he was clad in the rough clothing of the common laborer, he wore them with an air that even so exalted a personage as Sir Valerian might have envied. He carried a bulging valise, which indicated that he intended to stay. Daphne was not quite sure whether this was a good thing, or a bad one.

"I, er, I beg your pardon," he said, his green-eyed gaze shifting from Daphne to her mother and back again. "Have I come to the right place? I was told I might hire a room here."

"Yes, of course," Daphne said quickly, suddenly aware that she was staring. "We have several rooms vacant at the moment. How long do you plan to stay with us?"

"I don't know, exactly," he confessed with a shrug. "It might be as long as several months. I—I've taken a position at the mill."

"Oh," she said, conscious of a pang of disappointment. A mill worker, then. And yet his speech was not like that of the mill workers, at least not any of those with whom she had come in contact. A gentleman fallen on hard times, perhaps? They must be very hard times indeed, if he was forced to seek employment in a cotton mill rather than securing a more genteel position as a land steward, or a tutor, or even a clerk.

"In that case, you'll be wanting one of the less expensive rooms," her mother deduced, giving Daphne a nudge. "Don't just stand there, my love. Give me those linens, and then show our guest up to the Pennine Room. Dinner is served promptly at seven o'clock, Mr.—?"

"Tisdale. Theo Tisdale," he said, offering her mother a handshake. He wore no gloves, Daphne noted. His hands were well-shaped, and although Daphne would not call them soft, she could not bring herself to believe they had ever done a day's labor in their life.

"Mr. Tisdale," Mrs. Drinkard echoed. "As I say, dinner is served at seven, so you'll have time to wash up after work and put off your dirty clothes before joining us. Of course, you may make your own dining arrangements if you wish, which will reduce the cost of your room by sixpence per week. But my daughter will tell you all about that," she concluded, taking the sheets from Daphne's arms and shooing her toward the once-grand central staircase.

"The Pennine Room is the smallest, and thus the least expensive of the rooms," Daphne explained, leading the way up the stairs and blushing for the threadbare carpet covering the treads. "It lets for one-and-six per week, but that does include breakfast and dinner, as Mama says, in addition to washing your linens every Friday. If you choose to dispense with dining or laundry services, it brings the cost of the room down to a shilling—or sixpence, if you choose to forego both."

They had reached the top of the stairs by this time, and it seemed to Daphne that Mr. Tisdale let out a sigh of relief as she turned and started down the corridor.

"At least you're not putting me up in the attic," he

remarked.

"No, for the attic is set up as a kind of ward. Cots are available for tuppence the night, but no meals are included, nor any washing." She took a deep breath. "Mama meant no offense. I daresay she did not mention the attic because she thought it likely that you were accustomed to having a room of your own."

He gave a bitter little laugh. "She's in the right of it," he said cryptically, but offered no particulars. "Have you any other, er, guests staying here?"

"Not guests so much as permanent residents. Mrs. Jennings is an elderly lady who came to us after her husband died—her room is at the opposite end of the corridor from the one to which I'm taking you. Old Mr. Nethercote has the room directly across the corridor from yours. He is quite deaf, you see, and so is unlikely to be troubled by any noise from the dining room directly below." She glanced uncertainly up at him. "The Pennine Room is above the dining room as well, since it stretches from the front of the house to the back. That is, the dining room does, not the Pennine Room. I—I hope you will not be troubled by the noise. I daresay you will not—that is, I rather thought—"

"You thought I would come back from the mill so exhausted that I would collapse into bed and fall asleep regardless of any racket from below," deduced Mr. Tisdale. "You're very likely right. But I have to wonder exactly what goes on in the dining room that might disturb my sleep. Surely if there's a meal being served, I'll be in the dining room myself, contributing to the commotion."

"Yes, but there are the preparations to be made—setting the table for breakfast, and of course clearing away the dishes after dinner. And tomorrow night, a gentleman has hired the room for holding a meeting."

"A gentleman?" he echoed sharply. "Who?"

"His name is Sir Valerian Wadsworth. He is standing for Parliament, so I daresay it is some sort of political gathering. He wishes to meet with some of the mill workers."

"He'll catch cold at that," predicted Mr. Tisdale. "He'd do better to concentrate his efforts on men who are able to vote."

"Perhaps I misunderstood," Daphne conceded doubtfully. "I'm afraid I don't know much about politics. In any case, if they make too much noise, you must tell me. We cannot allow him to disturb our residents, no matter how much he may be paying Mama."

"Are we the only residents, then? Me, and this Mrs. Jennings and Mr.—Nethercoast, was it?"

"Nethercote," she corrected him gently. "But the three of you are not the only ones, for the curate also lives with us, and a solicitor's apprentice moved in about six months ago. Those are our only permanent residents. The others are usually men who have business at the mill—not mill workers, you understand, but men who have come to repair the equipment, vendors of dyestuffs—that sort of thing." In fact, the most recent of these had attempted more than once to catch her alone in the corridor and kiss her, but that unpleasant incident was none of Mr. Tisdale's business. She wondered if he were the sort of man who would try to corner a defenseless young woman, and wondered which would be the greater disappointment: to discover that he was, or to deduce, in the absence of any definitive evidence, that he was not.

They had by this time reached the room that bore on its paneled door a small plate reading "Pennine." Daphne turned the key in the lock and opened the door, then stepped back to allow him to survey the room that was to be his home for the foreseeable future. It was small, as she had said, but it had its own fireplace, and the narrow bed boasted a headboard of burnished brass. He set his valise down beside a chest of drawers positioned adjacent to the window, which looked out over the front of the house.

"There are larger rooms, but they are all occupied at present," Daphne offered apologetically, although precisely what she was apologizing for, she could not have said.

"This will do well enough," he conceded, withdrawing a coin purse from the inside pocket of his coat and counting out sufficient coins to cover the first week's lodging. "Now, is there somewhere I might find a drop to tide me over until dinner?"

"The Red Lion is not far away—perhaps a quarter of a mile," she said, gesturing in the direction he must travel to find this establishment.

"But not here?"

"My mother and I are not running a tavern, Mr. Tisdale," she informed him, very much on her dignity. "You may have coffee with your breakfast, half a glass of wine at dinner, and one cup of tea in the afternoon, if you should happen to be here when it is served."

"No, of course not. I beg your pardon. Now, if you will excuse me, I will see you at dinner," he said, and betook himself from the room.

But Daphne stood in the middle of the Pennine Room for a long time after he had gone, gazing speculatively at the door through which he had passed.

6

For I must to the greenwood go,
Alone, a banished man.
ANONYMOUS, *The Nut-Brown Maid*

Theodore was surprised and not a little indignant to find,
upon his return from the Red Lion, that his valise still sat
on the floor beside the chest of drawers, exactly as he had left
it. A moment's reflection, however, was sufficient to remind
him that he no longer had a valet to see to the unpacking of
his bags. Heaving a sigh, he picked up the valise and put it on
the bed, then set about removing his clothes to the chest of
drawers. By the time he had finished this task, it was time to
wash and change for dinner. No, he amended mentally, *not*
change. He hadn't brought a set of evening clothes with him,
and even if he had, he would have looked a pretty fool,
togging himself out in full evening kit to dine with a collection
of shabby-genteel mushrooms. He'd have to settle for
brushing what dust he could from the tailcoat he'd worn on
the stage—an unprepossessing garment of brown serge, fully
ten years old and bearing a small round hole, almost like a

bullet hole, near the top of one sleeve—and washing his face and hands before putting it back on to wear to dinner.

Alas, the pitcher on the washstand was empty—as he discovered when he attempted to pour hot water from it into the ceramic bowl provided for that purpose—and he glanced about the room in vain for a bellpull with which he might ring for a servant. He stepped out into the corridor, and almost collided with an elderly man in an old-fashioned bag wig, who cradled a pitcher to his chest with one hand while he fumbled for his room key with the other.

"I say," Theodore addressed this worthy, his eyes alighting on the pitcher, "Have you hot water there?"

"Eh?" asked the old man. "What's that?"

Clearly, this was the deaf Mr. Nethercote. "Hot water?" Theodore said again.

"No," his fellow houseguest informed him in the too-loud accents of the hard of hearing. "If you mean Miss Drinkard, she ain't my daughter."

"Not daughter; water," reiterated Theodore, raising his voice to match Mr. Nethercote's in volume. "Is that hot water in your pitcher?"

"Lud, no! If I were any richer, d'ye think I'd be living here?" retorted the old man, eyeing Theodore with disfavor. "Besides, ain't the sort of thing ye ought to be asking a stranger. Not much for manners, are ye?"

"All I want is some hot water!" shouted Theodore in some exasperation.

"Well, why didn't you say so?" grumbled Mr. Nethercote. "You want hot water, you'll have to go down to the kitchen and get it."

Muttering under his breath, Theodore returned to his room and grabbed the empty pitcher from its resting place in the bowl. When he returned to the corridor, Mr. Nethercote was still there, fumbling with his room key. Heaving a sigh of annoyance, Theodore snatched the key from the old man's hand, inserted it in the lock, and pushed the door open.

"There!" he pronounced, returning the key to his housemate before setting off in the direction of the staircase.

"Hair?" Mr. Nethercote echoed, putting a hand to his wig as he watched the younger man go. "Haven't worn my own hair in fifty years!" Shaking his head over the vagaries of the younger generation, he entered his room and closed the door behind him.

Theodore, meanwhile, went down the stairs to the ground floor of the house and glanced about for any sign of Miss Drinkard or her mother. Finding neither, he had no choice but to try and find the kitchen on his own. Fortunately, this was not difficult; having grown up in one of the stately homes of England, he had a very good idea of the general arrangement of such houses. It was only a matter of locating the green baize door that led from the house proper down to the servants' domain below. Having accomplished this, he had only to follow the clamor that indicated dinner preparations were in full swing.

He peered around the door whence most of the noises seemed to emanate. Sure enough, a mouthwatering aroma wafted from a large pot suspended over the fire from one of several cranes built into the fireplace for that purpose. At a stout deal table nearby, a squat middle-aged woman in a voluminous apron and mobcap dismembered a chicken by means of a carving knife wielded with one beefy arm as she simultaneously barked orders at two serving girls. No, Theodore amended mentally, one serving girl. The other apron-clad female was Miss Drinkard, stirring something in an earthenware bowl with a wooden spoon. Her cheeks were flushed with heat from the great fireplace, and wisps of brown hair escaped their pins to curl riotously about her temples and the nape of her neck.

"Er, excuse me," Theodore began tentatively.

"Oh! Mr. Tisdale!" exclaimed Miss Drinkard. If it were possible, her cheeks grew still redder. "What—? How may I—?"

"I'm sorry to disturb you," he said, unaccountably embarrassed at having discovered the daughter of the house engaged in a task better suited to the lowliest kitchen maid. "It's only—I was told that—I need hot water, you see, and Mr. Nethercote said—"

"Of course," she said quickly, abandoning her spoon in order to take the empty pitcher from him. "I should have told you when I showed you to your room. Water is kept on the hob all day, so you may fill your pitcher any time you have need of it."

She took a ladle from its hook by the fireplace and filled the pitcher with hot water from a large black cauldron. Theodore took careful note of her actions, reserving the knowledge against the following morning, when he would be expected to perform this task for himself. Finally, he took the pitcher from her, begged pardon once more for interrupting the meal preparations, and retreated up the two flights of stairs to his room. The pitcher was considerably heavier now, and he took care not to spill its contents onto the carpet even as he acknowledged that this could certainly do with a thorough cleaning.

In truth, the coming dinner gave him cause for considerable perturbation of spirits. A curate, Miss Drinkard had said, and a lawyer's apprentice, along with a couple of old people no doubt gentle of birth, but with pockets to let. He'd met Mr. Nethercote, and had been relieved to find that gentleman, at least, a total stranger. A curate, however, might well be cause for concern, as this young clergyman would no doubt have been educated at Oxford—where Theodore himself had matriculated, although not even the most charitable of his tutors there could have called his scholastic career anything but mediocre. A lawyer's apprentice was another possibility, although a somewhat less likely one. Then, too, there was Mrs. Jennings. How old was she, and was it possible that she had known his parents in their younger days? His memories of his mother were dim, as the duchess had died while he was still quite young, but he was said to resemble her, in temperament as well as countenance.

He began to wish he'd made a greater effort to disguise his true identity. He'd taken his title—his former title, rather—as his surname, thinking there might be people who would, quite correctly, connect the family name of Radney with his sister's name before her marriage. But what if this curate fellow, or fledgling lawyer, recognized plain "Mr.

Tisdale" as the erstwhile "Lord Tisdale," having known him at school? Perhaps he would have done better to have concocted a name from whole cloth. He had considered it, but thought it not worth the risk of forgetting, and failing to answer to his own name.

For much the same reason, he'd chosen not to imitate the speech of his native Devon, although as a child he'd picked it up easily enough from the stable hands—had got a thrashing for it, too, he recollected with a grin, when he'd elected to demonstrate this talent for the edification of his father's dinner guests. But he'd thought it would be too hard to keep up such a pretense, remembering the peculiarities of the dialect while at the same time performing whatever unfamiliar tasks might be assigned to him at the mill.

He'd decided instead to adopt the persona of a gentleman who had suffered a reversal of fortune, deducing that this disguise had the advantage of allowing him to adhere, as nearly as possible, to the truth; it had been a favorite aphorism of his nursery governess that telling one lie always led to a network of further lies in order to maintain the first, until the whole thing eventually collapsed of its own weight. As he descended the stairs, however, he began to think wistfully that one or two well-chosen lies might not have been amiss.

Great was his relief when he entered the dining room to find—aside from the ladies and old Mr. Nethercote—not one familiar face amongst the lot. Seats were not assigned, but his fellow diners' careful adherence to the rules of precedence gave evidence of genteel upbringing. He wondered fleetingly what had happened to them all that might account for their present reduced circumstances.

Mrs. Drinkard presided over the head of the table just as if she were hosting an elegant dinner party, while her daughter occupied the foot, arrayed in a blue satin gown that, if not quite in the first stare of fashion, nevertheless made it hard to believe she'd been employed in the kitchen scarcely an hour earlier. Mr. Nethercote, by virtue of his age, occupied the place of honor at his hostess's right, while Mrs. Jennings sat at Miss Drinkard's right, apparently for the same reason. The curate sat at Mrs. Drinkard's left, and Theodore was relieved to discover that this gentleman was at least forty years old, apparently languishing in his present position for lack of a patron; certainly he was too old to have known Theodore at Oxford, or Eton, or any of the other places where young men of noble birth might be expected to cross paths. The lawyer's apprentice was also a stranger, and one, furthermore, who glared at Theodore from his place at Miss Drinkard's left with much the same air as a dog guarding a bone. Theodore mumbled a greeting to the group at large, and took the chair between Mr. Nethercote and the curate.

"Good evening, Mr. Tisdale," said Mrs. Drinkard, inclining her head in a way that set the ostrich plumes in her hair bobbing. "Friends, this is Mr. Theodore Tisdale, who will be staying with us for a while. Mr. Tisdale, allow me to make you known to the other residents. Of course, you've met my daughter Daphne. This is Mrs. Mary Jennings, Mr. Edward Nethercote, Mr. Henry Nutley, and Mr. Thomas Potts."

As everyone was seated, nods sufficed in lieu of bows or curtseys, and the meal began. The dishes in their various serving vessels were already on the table, each one passed around hand to hand so that each boarder might take as much as he or she desired. Mrs. Drinkard explained to Theo that she preferred the presentation of dinner *à la française* to the growing fashion for service *à la russe*; Theo suspected, however, that her fondness for the earlier mode had more to do with a lack of footmen on hand to serve each person and then remove the dishes to make way for the next course.

"Tell me, Mr. Tisdale," said Mrs. Jennings, leaning a little forward in a way that put her long strand of pearls in danger of landing in her soup, "what brings you to Lancashire?"

It was the question he had been dreading, but he knew it could not be avoided. "I'll be taking a position at the mill in the morning," Theodore said repressively, daring anyone to ask for further enlightenment.

"Most mill workers live in the cottages on the other side of the river." The lawyer's apprentice sounded faintly accusatory, as if he suspected Theodore of taking up residence in the boardinghouse for the sole purpose of seducing Miss Drinkard. "They're closer to the mill."

"Then I suppose I'll have to be sure I get up early enough to walk," Theodore said blandly, and turned his attention to his dinner.

This proved to be a dish of chicken roasted with potatoes and seasoned with herbs—hardly surprising, since on his trek to the kitchen in search of water, he had seen the chicken and smelled the herbs. The result was a meal which, though woefully plain to one accustomed to elaborate concoctions devised by French chefs, was surprisingly good. Or perhaps it owed its appeal to the fact that Theodore had had nothing to eat since breakfast that morning. Either way, he addressed his plate with enthusiasm, until interrupted by Mr. Nutley, the curate.

"Wherever you choose to make your residence, Mr. Tisdale, I daresay you will find no cause for complaint in your employer. Sir Ethan Brundy is, I believe, a very good sort of man."

As Sir Ethan had fallen considerably in his brother-in-law's estimation over the past few days, Theodore offered no reply to this observation beyond a noncommittal grunt. Mr. Nethercote, however, was quick to fill what might otherwise have been an uncomfortable silence.

"Good leg of lamb?" he scoffed. "Balderdash! Anyone can see it's a chicken, Nutley. And a very good one, too," he added as an aside to his hostess.

"Why, thank you, Mr. Nethercote," said Mrs. Drinkard, turning quite pink with pleasure. "It is not always easy to set a pleasing meal on the table when I am so very pressed for— but never mind that! I shall convey your kind words to the cook."

The other diners, seeing how much this small tribute had meant to her, were quick to add their own praises. Once these compliments were conveyed, however, the curate returned to the subject of his original discourse.

"Yes, a very good sort of man, indeed," continued Mr. Nutley, blissfully unaware of having touched his fellow diner on the raw. "When Mr. Parsons—the vicar, you know, and very aptly named, is he not?—as I say, when Mr. Parsons made a very casual remark about how the church roof would need repairs before the winter sets in, scarcely a day had passed before Sir Ethan sent over a bank draft sufficient to cover the entire cost!"

Theodore was unimpressed with this proof of Sir Ethan's generosity, proving as it did that his brother by marriage might have settled Theodore's debts without the slightest inconvenience to himself, had he only chosen to do so. Once again, he was forced to bite his tongue in order to resist the urge to air his grievances.

"The boss, you say? Young Tisdale won't meet the boss tomorrow," objected Mr. Nethercote, who had at least grasped enough of the curate's speech to identify its subject. "Nor the day after that. Sir Ethan Brundy's gone to London."

"To London?" echoed Mrs. Drinkard. "Whatever is he doing in London in November? As I recall, the Metropolis is quite deserted this time of year. Everyone closes their town houses and returns to their country estates, or else they make up shooting parties." She heaved a reminiscent sigh for more prosperous days now gone forever. "What jolly times we used to have, riding to hounds across the countryside in the morning, and attending hunt balls at night!"

Miss Drinkard's eyes brightened at the mention of balls. "I believe Lady Helen Brundy gives a lovely autumn ball every year for her husband's workers. Not, of course," she added quickly, seeing her mother's frown, "that it is a ball in the sense that Mrs. Jennings and Mama will have known them, but—but it is a very nice gesture, is it not?"

"Nice enough for the mill workers, I daresay, but not the sort of thing you would enjoy at all, my love," her mother said repressively.

"No, Mama," Miss Drinkard said meekly, lowering her gaze to her plate.

Had she never been invited to these festivities, Theodore wondered, or did her mother not allow her to attend? He resolved to ask his sister to make sure Miss Drinkard received an invitation. Surely there could be nothing wrong with her going to the thing, so long as she was adequately chaperoned. It was clear enough that few pleasures came her way.

"Sir Ethan don't ride to hounds," said young Mr. Potts, "so there's no reason for him to remain in the country for such a reason as that. In fact, I believe he's gone to London to declare for the next Parliamentary election."

"Oh?" said Miss Drinkard, raising her dark eyes to him.

Finding himself in possession of all Miss Drinkard's attention, Mr. Potts sat up straighter in his chair and enlarged upon this theme. "Whig candidate. Standing for the Marquess of Cutliffe's seat. Cutliffe"—Theodore noticed that the lawyer's apprentice dropped the "Lord" designation, just as if he were personally acquainted with the marquess—"was obliged to give it up once he inherited the title from his elder brother. Peers can't sit in the Commons, you know."

"Who—who is his opponent?" Miss Drinkard asked with a valiant attempt at indifference betrayed only by her heightened color.

"Fellow named Wadsworth. Baronet, I believe."

"Sir Valerian Wadsworth?" asked Mrs. Drinkard. "Why,

he was here earlier today, wanting to hire the dining room tomorrow night for a meeting! Can it be a political gathering, do you suppose? But no, he spoke of a meeting for the workers, and they won't be able to vote."

At this recollection, her face fell so comically that Theodore wondered if she'd envisioned herself as a political hostess. It was interesting to note that, although her daughter was not to mingle socially with the mill workers, Mrs. Drinkard apparently had no qualms about throwing open her dining room to them. Sir Valerian Wadsworth must be paying her generously for its use. Still, Theodore would wager Miss Drinkard would be kept well out of sight of the gathering, lest she be corrupted by close proximity to the lower orders. Who the devil did her mother think she was saving her for—Mr. Potts? Mr. Nutley? Or, it occurred to him with dawning comprehension, the Parliamentary candidate himself? For that matter, why would this Sir Valerian Wadsworth have any interest in meeting with his opponent's workers in the first place? Good God! Just what sort of establishment had he wandered into?

7

Half the world knows not how the other half lives.
GEORGE HERBERT, *Jacula Prudentum*

Since his emancipation from Oxford two years previously, Theodore had formed the habit of staying out late and remaining abed until noon. It was not surprising, therefore, that he overslept the next morning, and was obliged to scramble into his new garments—new? His tailor would go off in an apoplexy at the sight of them!—before setting out for the mill, stopping in the dining room only long enough to grab a couple of rolls to eat along the way.

He crossed the stone bridge that arched over the river, giving him a glimpse of the mill that dominated the riverbank downstream, and recalled with mixed emotions that his brother by marriage had offered, more than once, to show him the inner workings of the manufactory that provided employment for most of the village and its environs. On the one hand, if he had taken Ethan up on the offer, he might have some idea of what he was walking into now; on the other hand, it was probably best that he had not, lest he be recognized by the workers. Then again, he had scarcely recognized himself in the vision that had met his eyes in the looking glass above the washstand: a tall, slender young man with unkempt blond hair, a faint golden stubble adorning his chin (he'd had no more time for shaving than he'd had for breakfast) and an unstarched cravat knotted about his neck beneath the limp collar of his loose smock.

Upon reaching the mill, he tugged open the heavy door and stepped inside. He blinked as his eyes, accustomed to a sun that seemed to smile in mockery upon his present dilemma, adjusted to the dimmer light inside. Rows of machines were ranged along both sides of a central aisle, each one operated by a man dressed very much as Theodore was. A few of the men looked up at his entrance, and Theodore stopped to address the nearest of these, raising his voice to be heard over the din of the machines.

"Good morning!" he bellowed. "I'd like to speak to the foreman."

The man shook his head, and shouted back, "Won't find him here. Gone to London, he has."

"He might have told me," Theodore grumbled under his breath.

"Eh?" the man asked, cupping a hand about his ear. "What's that?"

"Sir E—that is, I was told I might speak to Abel Wilkins about a position here," Theodore said, raising his voice once more.

"Well, why didn't you say so?" He jerked his head toward the rear of the cavernous room. "You'll find him back there, in the foreman's office. He's not the foreman, mind; that would be his son-in-law, Tommy Crenshaw. But Tommy's gone to London—something about a new hand—lost his own years ago, you know—and so Wilkins is acting foreman until he gets back."

Theodore could only consider this a good thing, as he vaguely recalled an earlier visit to Ethan and Helen during which he'd been introduced to Tommy and his wife—this man Wilkins's daughter, he supposed—at church. Church! Good God! Would the vicar remember him?

Aloud, Theo merely thanked the man and made his way down the aisle and into another room (this one filled with yet another kind of machine that emitted a high-pitched whine) until he reached the rear of the building. One corner had been walled off to form a small room, with unglazed windows cut into its walls to allow anyone inside to look out into the mill itself—and anyone in the mill to look inside the office, where a man sat behind a desk, leaning back in his chair with his feet propped up amongst the papers stacked neatly on the surface of the desk. Despite the fact that he might have shouted for the fellow's attention, Theodore knocked on the door and waited for the man, presumably Mr. Wilkins, to admit him. Not that Wilkins (assuming it was he) appeared in any hurry to do so. He sat upright and spat a wad of tobacco into a spittoon, then heaved himself to his feet and crossed the small room, disappearing from Theodore's line of sight for a moment before reappearing as he opened the door.

"Well?" he asked, looking Theodore up and down with an expression of suspicion not unmixed with hostility. "What d'you want?"

"Wilkins?" Theodore responded. "Abel Wilkins?"

The foreman—no, *acting* foreman—folded beefy arms across his chest and leaned against the doorjamb. "What if I am?"

"Ethan—that is, Sir Ethan Brundy offered me a position in the mill." It hadn't happened exactly that way, of course, but that was all the explanation Theodore intended to give. "He told me to present myself to a man named Wilkins."

"That's *Mr.* Wilkins to you," the older man retorted, having apparently taken Theodore in instant dislike. He looked about him for the spittoon and, finding it absent, spat on the floor instead. "And you are?"

"Tisdale. Theodore Tisdale," said Theo, offering his hand.

Mr. Wilkins looked a bit taken aback by this gesture, but took the proffered hand. " 'Theodore,' is it? Lily-white hands won't look like that for long," he predicted grimly. "So, I'm supposed to find a place for you, eh? Oh, all right then, come along."

He strode back the way Theodore had come, leaving the younger man to keep up—or not. Stopping at last before the machines Theodore had seen upon first entering the mill, he raised his voice to be heard over the noise issuing from them. "You can start here. Tom here will show you the ropes."

He jerked his head in the direction of the fellow manning the nearest machine, a middle-aged man with a ruddy complexion and a cheerful disposition, as evidenced by the way he whistled as he went about his task of feeding thread into the machine. "Tom, this here's Tisdale. Thee-o-dore Tisdale," he added, making a mockery of a name which, Theodore had to admit, sounded rather too grandiose for his present surroundings.

"How do you do?" Theodore started to offer his hand, then realized Tom's hands were occupied, and settled for giving the man a nod. "But please, call me Theo." He had no desire to assume the title by which he'd been known at first Eton and then Oxford, but neither did he wish to be called by his nursery sobriquet of "Teddy."

Tom nodded back. "Pleased to meet you, Theo. I'll take it from here, Mr. Wilkins," he added to the other man.

The acting foreman turned and left them, presumably to return to the office. Tom, watching him go, observed, "Wilkins don't much like you."

"It would appear not," Theo concurred.

"Got any idea why?"

Theo shook his head. "None. If I offered some insult, it was not intentional, I assure you."

"Never you mind," Tom said with a shrug. "With Wilkins, it don't take much. Still, I'd watch my back, if I was you. It's not what you'd call healthy to get on his bad side."

"Meaning?" prompted Theo.

"Never mind," Tom said again, casting a furtive glance 'round, as if he feared Wilkins might be eavesdropping. In quite another tone, he added, "Now, first thing, you'd best get rid of that neck-wipe."

"What, my cravat?" Theo asked, his hand going instinctively to the strip of limp white linen knotted about his neck. It had been difficult achieving even this inferior result with an unstarched neckcloth. He wasn't sure another attempt—and one, moreover, without the aid of a mirror—would be any more successful. He was about to say so when he realized that not one of the men within his immediate line of vision wore a neckcloth at all. Instead, the collars of their shirts were open, each one displaying a bare "V" of flesh that already glistened with perspiration even though the day's work had scarcely begun.

"Too great a risk of it being grabbed and pulled into the loom. Trust me," Tom added darkly, "you don't want that to happen."

Theo did not have to be told twice. Suppressing a shudder at the grisly possibility raised by Tom's warning, he untied the floppy knot and stuffed the strip of cloth into the waistband of his breeches—in the back, where it would be safe from the hungry maw of the power loom. He might look a bit ridiculous—rather as if he had a tail—but surely this was better than the alternative. In any case, he had the lowering conviction that he would make a bigger fool of himself than this relatively minor infraction before the day was over.

Tom proved to be as good as his word, instructing Theo in the most efficient way to feed the flying shuttle without getting his fingers pinched or, worse, his hair or clothing trapped. Even while he absorbed this information, however, Theo's thoughts returned to his brother by marriage. Whatever else might be said of him (and Theo had said quite a lot over the last few days, none of it flattering), Ethan was a shrewd judge of character. It seemed unlike him to leave his mill in the charge of a bully-boy whose subordinates seemed to tread in fear of him. Did Ethan not know? Perhaps Wilkins showed the owner of the mill quite a different face than the one the men beneath him saw; perhaps the workers were afraid to let on, for fear of reprisals once Ethan returned to London. Should Theo somehow get word to him, and let him know how things stood?

He had not long to ponder this dilemma, however, for once Tom returned to his own machine, leaving Theo to fend for himself, that young man had all he could handle just keeping up with his work. The loom was much faster than he had expected, grabbing the thread as fast as—or faster than—he could feed it in. By the end of two hours, the pads of his thumbs and the sides of his index fingers were reddened and sore from the cotton fibers sliding between them; by the end of four, several blisters had formed. When he was finally able to stop for a midday meal, he realized with some chagrin that, in his haste to reach the mill on time, he had neglected to provide himself with anything to eat.

As the workers left their stations and filed into an adjoining room furnished with long tables and benches, Theo followed in their wake, trying to act as if he was not hungry at all. He took a seat on the nearest bench, sitting with the table at his back so that he might rest his spine against it. Unfortunately, it soon appeared that his seeming nonchalance did not fool anyone.

"Never mind, lad, it gets better with time."

Turning to identify the speaker, Theo found him in the man seated on the opposite side of the table. He might have been any age between fifty and seventy, although if his wrinkled face and missing teeth were anything to judge by, Theo thought it was nearer the latter. Still, in spite of his unprepossessing countenance, his eyes were kind, and his smile (gap-toothed though it was) held nothing of mockery.

"I hope you're right," Theo said, hoping even more fervently that he would not remain at the mill long enough to find out if the old man's prediction was correct. He swung his long legs over the bench and underneath the table, the better to offer his hand to the encouraging stranger. "How do you do? Theo Tisdale's the name. And you are—?"

"Benjamin Yates. But you can call me Old Ben. Everyone else does." He glanced down at the blistered hand clasping his. "You'll want to get some bandages on those before tomorrow. Won't do to have you bleeding all over the cloth."

Theo grinned mischievously at him. "I don't know about that. It might serve—well, never mind that," he amended hastily.

Old Ben cast a quick glance around the room and then leaned forward, lowering his voice to a conspiratorial whisper. "Might serve Wilkins right? Aye, maybe it would, at that. But you don't want to go setting up his back, you know."

In fact, Wilkins had not been uppermost in Theo's thoughts, but it recalled to his mind the circumstance he had wondered at earlier. "No, of course not. Tom said as much. But tell me, why has no one mentioned the matter to E—to Sir Ethan Brundy? He wouldn't—that is, he doesn't seem the sort of man who would tolerate such a thing, if he knew of it."

"Aye, you've the right of it there. But Wilkins's nose was put out of joint when our Ethan"—Theodore noticed Old Ben didn't bother to use his brother-in-law's title—"up and married the daughter of a duke, when he'd had hopes there for his daughter Becky."

To Theo, who had seen the *beau monde* react to that same marriage with revulsion, it came as a considerable shock to discover that, in some circles, Ethan Brundy had been seen as a very eligible *parti*. "Becky," he echoed thoughtfully. "But she married someone else, didn't she? The foreman?"

"Aye, she were already mad for Tommy, and he for her. Ethan gave Tommy a rise in wages, to make him a mite easier for Wilkins to swallow as a son-in-law—him having lost an arm, you know, and Wilkins saying he won't give his girl to a cripple—and then he made Wilkins assistant foreman, thinking that might smooth his ruffled feathers."

"Did it?" asked Theo, intrigued in spite of himself by this hitherto unsuspected result of his sister's marriage.

Old Ben shook his head. "Not that I could tell."

"But, dash it, it's been four years!" exclaimed Theo, unwittingly betraying far too intimate a knowledge of his employer's marriage. "Surely if he was capable of being placated, it would have happened by now."

"Aye, you're probably right."

"Then why doesn't someone speak up?"

One graying eyebrow lifted toward Old Ben's hairline. "Are you volunteering for the job?"

Theo started to make a hasty demurral, but reconsidered. Surely no one was in a better position than he to make Ethan aware of how matters stood. "Maybe I am, at that," he said thoughtfully.

Old Ben reached across the table and laid a hand on Theo's arm as if to forestall him. "Take my advice, lad. Don't do it. Oh, I know you mean well," he added quickly, anticipating Theo's objection. "But it won't serve. You'll only make a deal of trouble for all of us."

"But Sir Ethan needs to know," Theo insisted.

"Aye, but think, lad. Ethan can't stay here forever. His lady wife likes London—and he likes his lady wife too much to disappoint her. Then, too, he's standing for Parliament. Soon or late, he'll return to London, and as soon as he's gone—" He drew a hand across his neck.

Theo did not interpret this gesture literally—he doubted that any throats would be slit—but understood it to mean that Wilkins's vengeance against the informer would be swift and sure.

"But you're not eating," Ben protested in a very different voice, his shrewd gaze falling on the empty expanse of table before Theo.

Theo shrugged in a not entirely successful attempt at nonchalance. "I—I'm not really hungry," he lied.

"You will be, by the end of the day," predicted Ben with the confidence of long experience. "Here, take some of this."

He tore off a large piece of bread from his loaf and handed it across the table. A hunk of cheese and an apple followed the bread.

"I can't take your food!" Theo protested, although his neglected stomach growled in anticipation.

Hearing this, Ben's knowing gaze dropped to Theo's middle. "Your belly says otherwise."

"Yes, well, I forgot—I overslept this morning, and barely had breakfast. I forgot that I would need something for the middle of the day."

"You won't forget again," Ben said reassuringly. "You'll remember to bring something tomorrow, but until then, you'd do best to take this. We've five more hours yet, you know."

"Five more hours," echoed Theo in failing accents.

"Could be worse," Ben pointed out. "One of the first things our Ethan did when he inherited the mill was cut working hours from fourteen to ten."

Alas, Theo could not share Ben's enthusiasm for "our Ethan's" generosity. By the end of the day, his back ached and his hands throbbed, several of the blisters by this time having broken open. He wanted nothing more than to collapse onto his own bed (or what passed for his own bed, at least for the nonce) and sleep the clock 'round. Instead, he would have to get up at dawn the next morning and do it all again. He was denied even the luxury of a brief nap, however, for upon entering the boarding house, he was met at the door by Mrs. Drinkard, who urged him to hurry and wash up for dinner.

"For we must dine a bit early tonight, in order to set the dining room to rights for tonight's political meeting," she explained, clearly in some agitation lest the location Sir Valerian had chosen for his meeting should fail to find favor in the Parliamentary hopeful's eyes.

Theo glanced over her shoulder at Miss Drinkard, who was engaged in arranging chrysanthemums in a bowl that stood on the small table in the foyer. She wore a coarse cotton apron over the same blue satin gown she'd worn to dinner the previous evening, this time enhanced with a single strand of pearls which contrasted jarringly with the apron. He wondered if this added touch was in anticipation of Sir Valerian's visit— and, if so, whether it had been her own idea or her mother's. As if aware of his scrutiny, she looked up from her task and their eyes met in the mirror mounted on the wall over the table. Her lips curved in an apologetic little smile, and her eyes held a silent plea for understanding.

"Of course," Theo told his hostess. "I shall be back down directly." With this assurance, he gave the ladies a nod and betook himself up the stairs to his room.

Back in London, his dinner preparations would have included trading his buckskin breeches and blue tailcoat with its gleaming brass buttons for the form-fitting black panta-loons and black tailcoat deemed suitable for evening. Perhaps, he reflected for the second time in as many days, it was just as well that he'd brought no such garments with him; one could hardly scramble into one's evening clothes, and thanks to Sir Valerian and his political gathering, he would not have had sufficient time to turn himself out in style in any case.

Resolved to do the best he could in the time he had, he stripped off his sweat-soaked work clothing and poured water from the pitcher into the bowl. This would long since have grown cold, but if his presence had been very much *de trop* when he'd gone to the kitchen in search of it the previous evening, he suspected it would be doubly so tonight. He bathed himself with water that was just as cold as he'd expected, then arrayed himself in the same clothing he'd worn to dinner the previous evening; if it was acceptable for the daughter of the house to wear the same garments two nights running, he reasoned, then it must surely be so for one of the tenants.

Finally, he picked up his hairbrush and swept it through his golden locks—and muttered a curse under his breath at the cloud of lint produced by this simple act. He strode across the small room to the window, threw open the sash, and stuck his head out, then brushed his hair so that the resulting snowfall drifted to the ground below rather than onto the floor. Having finished with this task, he stripped off the brown tailcoat he'd just put on and, in the absence of a lint brush, shook it vigorously out the window before putting it back on and descending the stairs once more to the dining room.

Mrs. Drinkard's high hopes for the evening had apparently communicated themselves to the other residents, for it seemed to Theodore that all of them (all except himself, anyway) had gone out of their way to appear to advantage. Mr. Nethercote wore a crimson velvet coat that would have been the height of fashion in the last century, and Mrs. Jennings had chosen to air a set of garnets that might have been much improved by a thorough cleaning. Even Mr. Nutley's rusty black clerical garb appeared to have been painstakingly brushed, and Mr. Potts had attempted, not entirely successfully, to tie his cravat in a fashionable Waterfall.

"I should like to hear more about this political gathering, Mrs. Drinkard," urged the aspiring lawyer. "What is it all about?"

"Now, that's just what I don't know," confessed his hostess. "Sir Valerian said he wished to hire a room where he might meet with some of the mill workers. I daresay Mr. Tisdale can tell us more," she suggested, turning expectantly toward Theo.

He shook his head. "I don't know any more than you do. Less, in fact."

"But surely someone at the mill must have spoken of it!" exclaimed Mrs. Drinkard, clearly in some dismay that the meeting might prove not to be the brilliant *coup* she had hoped for.

"If they did, I never heard of it. But," he added quickly, seeing her distress, "recall that today was my first day there. It might be that the workers would not care to discuss a matter of such importance in front of a stranger."

"Yes, that is very likely the case," agreed Mrs. Drinkard, brightening a little. Belatedly realizing that this assumption was hardly flattering to her newest tenant, she added hastily, "Not, of course, that we don't know how very amiable you are, Mr. Tisdale, but the men at the mill will not be so well acquainted with you."

As she had known him scarcely more than twenty-four hours, Theo was hard pressed to hold back a grin. "I am obliged to you, ma'am," he said meekly, and had his reward when he glanced at Miss Drinkard to find her smiling gratefully at him.

Alas, this proved to be the one bright point of the evening meal. Holding his fork in his blistered hand proved to be an agony, and as the brisket of beef to which Mrs. Drinkard treated her guests that evening was somewhat tough, wielding his knife was even worse. As a result, he ate little in spite of his hunger, but excused himself from the table as soon as he could do so without giving offense, and returned to his room, where he wanted only to seek oblivion in Morpheus's embrace.

Unfortunately, he had reckoned without Sir Valerian's political gathering. He had hardly settled himself between the sheets before the first arrivals appeared, as evidenced by the sounds of tramping footsteps beneath his window, followed in quick succession by the rapping of the door knocker and Mrs. Drinkard's voice welcoming the mill workers with a careful blend of hospitality and condescension. That same voice assuming a very different tone was sufficient to inform him that Sir Valerian himself had arrived.

But Theo's troubles were only beginning. As his room was directly over the dining room, the sounds of the gathering drifted up the chimney flue, obliging him to pull first the covers and, finally, the pillow over his head in a futile attempt to muffle the voices that grew increasingly agitated as the meeting progressed. And then, quite suddenly, two words rose above the babel of voices, two words that caused Theo to throw off the pillow and bedclothes, and to sit bolt upright in his bed.

The words were "Ethan Brundy."

8

Listen for dear honor's sake.
JOHN MILTON, *Comus*

Theo crossed the small room in three strides. Kneeling before the fireplace (heedless of the discomfort to knees cushioned by nothing more than a thin cambric nightshirt), he thrust his head in, the better to hear the angry voices that drifted up through the flue. While the voices were not difficult to hear, distinguishing the words they spoke was quite another matter. The speakers often talked over one another, to such an extent that Theo wondered if the people in the room directly below could understand each other any better than he could understand them himself. Occasionally, however, a word or phrase made itself heard, and these were enough to fill him with foreboding: "Employer? Slave-driver, more like!" "—getting above himself—" "—while he lives like a king" and, most ominous of all, "—time to take action—"

Action? What sort of action? Theo instinctively leaned forward, as if by doing so he might more easily understand any specifics offered for putting this vague threat into practice. Alas, if any such specifics were put forward, Theo never heard them, for he was distracted at that moment by a light knock on his door.

He jerked upright, and cracked his head on the brick lintel. Muttering imprecations under his breath (although whether these were directed toward the unyielding lintel or the uninvited caller, even he could not have said), he scrambled to his feet, ignoring the protests of his aching muscles.

"Coming!" he called, then snatched up the breeches he had discarded earlier and tugged them on, stuffing his nightshirt into the waistband. Having made himself decent, if not entirely presentable, he opened the door—and was stunned to see Miss Drinkard standing in the corridor just beyond the threshold, bearing a tray with a bowl of steaming water, a jar of some unguent, a pair of scissors, and a roll of cotton lint. Theo eyed this last with disfavor. If he never saw a shred of cotton again, it would be all too soon.

"I—I'm sorry to disturb you," she stammered, blushing a little at the sight of his *déshabille*.

"Well, now that you have, what do you want?" Annoyed and more than a little embarrassed at being interrupted in the act of eavesdropping, Theo spoke perhaps a bit more sharply than the situation warranted.

"It was nothing. Just—I beg your pardon—I should not have—"

She began to back away, and Theo instantly regretted his show of temper. "No, don't go. I'm a brute to lash out at you. It's just that, well, it's been a hard day." As if in proof of this statement, he raked one abused hand through his disheveled golden curls.

"Yes, I'm sure it must have been," she said, halting in mid-flight. "That was why I came. I noticed you weren't eating much at dinner, and saw—" She made a helpless little gesture toward his hands, and tried again. "Mama keeps a supply of basilicum ointment in the stillroom, and I thought you might need some."

"And for this, I snapped your head off," said Theo, filled with remorse. "It was kind of you to think of me. I would be glad of any assistance you would care to offer—although if you've changed your mind after the rude welcome I gave you, it will be no more than I deserve."

Miss Drinkard hastily denied having any such thought in her head, and Theo invited her inside—being careful, of course, to nudge the doorstop in place with his foot in order to satisfy the demands of propriety by keeping the door open. She gave him a shy smile at his ready understanding of the potential awkwardness of her situation, then commanded him to take a seat on the room's only chair, the one positioned before the writing desk. He obeyed this behest, albeit not before taking the tray from her—ignoring her protests that he must consider his poor hands—and setting it on the desk.

"First, you must turn up your sleeves," she cautioned him as she plunged a cloth into the bowl of hot water. "The nights have grown quite chilly, and you will not want to sleep in a wet shirt."

Theo submitted to these instructions with a good grace, rolling his sleeves up halfway to the elbows and revealing a pair of forearms lightly dusted with golden hair. "Tell me,

Miss Drinkard, does it often fall to your lot to act as physician to your mother's tenants?"

"Mama prefers to call them guests," she confided, lowering her voice. "It is all a pretense, of course, but one can't really blame her. As for my acting as their physician, I wouldn't say it occurs 'often,' but it is not unusual. Just last winter, poor Mrs. Jennings was so ill with the influenza that we feared we might lose her. Mama did not quite like me tending her, for fear I should fall ill myself, but I couldn't bear to see the poor old dear suffer so." She wrung the excess water from the cloth, then set about dabbing away the dried blood that had crusted about the worst of Theo's blisters. "And then there was the time I was obliged to splint poor Mr. Potts's arm until the surgeon could be sent for."

"I expect he enjoyed that," Theo remarked drily. In fact, he was aware of a certain pleasurable sensation himself. Miss Drinkard's hands were gentle on his, and he found himself wondering what it might be like were she to touch him for reasons unrelated to the practice of medicine. Gentle, certainly, but if her labors in the kitchen were anything to judge by, then possessing a surprising strength as well . . .

She looked up abruptly from her work. "Oh, so you noticed that, did you?"

Theo gave a guilty start. "What? Oh—yes—Mr. Potts. Well—forgive me, Miss Drinkard, but he makes it rather difficult not to."

She gave a little huff of annoyance. "I have told him he must not—must not entertain hopes in that direction. Even if I were to—to return his very flattering sentiments, Mama would never countenance such a match." She glanced up from her work, giving him a glimpse of speaking dark eyes before lowering them once more. "Mr. Potts is not the only one to entertain hopes, you know, and Mama has not entirely abandoned hers. She wants to see me make a brilliant match."

He had guessed as much, of course, and yet was taken aback nevertheless at hearing it so baldly stated. "I don't mean to sound disrespectful, Miss Drinkard, but in your present situation, such an outcome seems unlikely."

"Yes, I know."

"Under the circumstances, I daresay the arrival of Sir Valerian must seem like a godsend," observed Theo.

By this time she had finished cleaning his blistered hands and had progressed to swabbing them with the basilicum ointment, but at the mention of Sir Valerian, her gaze shifted to the fireplace, from whence indistinct voices could still be heard. "Yes, but although Mama could not but welcome the extra money, Sir Valerian must not be allowed to inconvenience the other guests. If the noise from his meetings will disturb you, he must find somewhere else to host them."

"*No!* Er, that is, no," said Theo, modulating his tone. "I daresay it will be just as you predicted, and I shall be able to sleep through any disturbance, now that my hands will no longer pain me. It is very kind of you, Miss Drinkard."

"Surely we're not back to *that!*" protested Daphne, deftly unwinding a length of cotton lint.

"Back to what?" asked Theo, all at sea.

She bent upon him a roguish smile with a dimple at the corner of her mouth. "Your telling me how kind I am, and my assuring you that it is nothing at all." In a more serious vein, she added, "I am often lonely, Mr. Tisdale. You seem to have some understanding of my predicament, and yet you do not seek to placate my pride by mouthing well-meaning platitudes. I had thought perhaps we might be—friends."

"I am sure Mrs. Drinkard would say I am not at all a proper 'friend' for you to have."

"Yes, but Mama does not—does not understand," she confessed, albeit a bit grudgingly. "She would say you are only a mill worker, and that you are not a proper person for me to know."

"And what does Miss Drinkard say?"

She picked up the scissors and sliced through the cotton lint, then gave him a long and searching look. "I think you and I might understand one another very well, for we have something in common, do we not?"

"Do we?" he asked warily.

"Come, Mr. Tisdale, it must be obvious to the meanest intelligence that you are no ordinary mill worker! You are, or were, a gentleman, although you appear to have fallen on hard times. Deny it, if you can!"

Theo shrugged in resignation. "Very well, Miss Drinkard. There you have me. I have fallen on *very* hard times. Still, I have hopes of bringing myself about very soon."

She gave him a look of sympathetic understanding. "It never entirely goes away, does it?"

"Does what?"

"Hope. No matter how impossible things seem, we can't quite let it go. Mama, with her confidence that I may yet repair our fortunes by making a brilliant match even while living in a boardinghouse, your expectations of bringing yourself about by working in a cotton mill—" Her eyes grew round as a new thought occurred to her. "But wait! Perhaps there is a chance for you, after all!"

"Oh?"

"Perhaps Sir Valerian might be persuaded to engage you as his secretary!" Her eagerness gave way to mild indignation as Theo gave a shout of laughter. "What have I said that was so funny?"

"Nothing—pay me no heed," he said, struggling to control his mirth. "It's just that I am the last man on earth Sir Valerian would want as his secretary."

"Are you, indeed?" she asked, somewhat deflated by this revelation. "Are you so well acquainted with him?"

"Never met the fellow in my life," declared Theo.

"Well, then—!"

"Let us just say that there are reasons why I am unsuited to such a position," Theo amended. "Still, it was very wrong of me to laugh at you. You are very kind to want to help me."

"If you're back to telling me how kind I am, I shall go." She tied off her neat bandage with a tug just a bit harder than was strictly necessary, then piled her various accoutrements back on the tray, picked it up, and flounced across the room, reminding Theo of nothing so much as an outraged kitten. Having reached the door, she turned back to add, albeit grudgingly, "There is some beef left over from dinner. Cook has shredded it up for a pie, but if you would like a bit of it to take to the mill tomorrow for a noon meal, you may have it, along with some bread and cheese. And now, I shall bid you goodnight, before you can tell me again how kind I am!"

And with this parting shot, she closed the door with a snap. Theo sat grinning at the uncommunicative door for a long moment before remembering his interrupted mission. Alas, the meeting had apparently concluded, for no more sounds could be heard through the flue. He supposed he should be disappointed at not being able to discover more of exactly what Sir Valerian thought he was about, but he could not entirely regret it—and if the truth were known, his lack of repentance was not wholly due to the condition of his hands, although there was no denying that these did feel rather better as a result of Miss Drinkard's ministrations.

It occurred to him that he might learn as much of Sir Valerian's doings from Miss Drinkard as he did through the chimney flue. After all, Mrs. Drinkard would only encourage any interaction between her daughter and the Parliamentary candidate, certain that such an exchange could only end in the banns being posted. And if Miss Drinkard wished to confide the details of these conversations to her sympathetic "friend," well, who was he to deny her? He might even ask her to put in a good word for him with Sir Valerian; the absurdity of his taking a position as secretary to his brother-in-law's opponent appealed to him, whether or not he was ever offered the post Miss Drinkard had proposed.

He snuffed the candle and crawled back into bed, feeling lighter at heart than he had in many a long day—since, in fact, the night his father had died.

* * *

Alas for Theo, his more cheerful frame of mind scarcely survived the night. Waking at dawn for his second day on the job proved to be no problem; in fact, his aching muscles jolted him from sleep every time he rolled over. This circumstance did at least guarantee that he had time to shave and even eat a bowl of porridge dipped from a kettle of this concoction kept on the hob, as Mrs. Drinkard's more elderly "guests" kept to the late mornings they had enjoyed in more prosperous times.

"Thankee," said the cook when Theo returned his bowl to the kitchen for washing. In truth, she was a bit taken aback by this show of consideration, as the dirty dishes were usually left on the table for Miss Daphne to fetch down later in the morning. She wondered if it was to ingratiate himself with the daughter of the house that he'd performed this small task for her. Well, he'd catch cold at that, as he'd learn before he was much older. The newest resident might be a pretty-behaved young man—aye, and a good-looking one too, she'd grant him that—but it wouldn't do for Miss Daphne to go entertaining hopes in that direction. Still, she unbent sufficiently to look up from the dough she was kneading and jerk her head in the direction of a wicker basket covered with a gingham cloth. "Miss Daphne said you was to have that."

"Oh?" Theo lifted a corner of the cloth and found the remains of the beef Miss Drinkard had mentioned, now shredded and stuffed between thick hunks of bread along with a paper-thin slice of cheddar.

"Aye, she thought you might get hungry, working at the mill all day," Cook said, pounding one beefy fist into the ball of dough.

Theo, correctly deducing that she would be only too happy to perform a similar operation on any man who failed to show "Miss Daphne" the proper degree of respect, thought it politic not to betray any hint of the late-night exchange that had resulted in this show of generosity.

"She was right. Will you please convey my thanks to her? Tell her I said it was kind of her to think of me," he added with a hint of a smile. He would convey his own thanks that evening, but in the meantime, it amused him to think of how she might receive a message once again referencing her kindness. He picked up the basket and set out, whistling, for the mill, his good humor quite restored.

Even had he not known of Sir Valerian's meeting, he would have recognized within ten minutes of his arrival that something had changed, and not for the better. An air of tension hung over the mill that had not been there the previous day. Small knots of men engaged in hushed conversations or exchanged furtive looks from their posts at the power looms. Others, like Tom, seemed even more wary than before, regarding their co-workers with distrust if not outright suspicion.

"Tom," Theo said at last, raising his voice only as much as necessary for the other man to hear him over the noise of the machines, "is something wrong?"

"Of course not!" Tom said a bit too quickly. "Why should there be anything wrong?"

"No particular reason," Theo said, trying to match the other man's attempt at nonchalance, and failing quite as miserably. "You just seem—distracted."

"Distraction is dangerous." As if to prove his point, Tom focused his gaze intently on the thread as he fed it into the loom. "The sooner you learn that, the safer you'll be."

Theo would have pressed him to elaborate, but was interrupted by the arrival of Wilkins. "What's toward, Tom? Is Thee-o-dore here bothering you?" Again, he made a mockery of Theo's given name.

"It's all right, Abel."

"What's that, Tom?" asked the foreman, taking a menacing step forward.

"It's all right, Mr. Wilkins," amended Tom in placating accents. "Theo just had a question, and I was answering it."

Wilkins turned his beady-eyed gaze on Theo. "You've got your answer, then. Now, get back to work, Tom. Not you," he added to Theo. "You come with me."

Theo did as he was told, following Wilkins back to the small room where he'd first had the dubious pleasure of making the man's acquaintance. As they traversed the mill, he could not help noticing the expressions on the faces of his fellow workers, expressions ranging from malicious to apprehensive to sympathetic. He was surprised, upon first entering the makeshift office, to discover that the desk was now covered with a white tablecloth. Upon closer inspection, he realized it was a length of the same cotton cloth that he was employed to produce.

"Aye, take a good look at it," commanded Wilkins, noting the direction of his gaze. "What d'you see?"

Thus ordered, Theo bent for a more thorough inspection, and noticed that certain threads were streaked with a reddish-brown substance.

"The stains," he said. "Are they—"

"Aye, they're your own blood," Wilkins said with malicious satisfaction. "Here's a piece of otherwise good cloth two ells long that can't be sold now, because someone's lily-white hands bled all over it. What do you suggest we do with it?"

Theo would have liked very much to tell Wilkins exactly what he could do with it, but quite aside from the fact that this would do nothing to make his life at the mill any easier, he was afraid the man had a point.

"I'm very sorry," he said at last. "As you noted, I'm not accustomed to the work, and rubbed blisters on my hands. I've come better prepared today, so it won't happen again." He lifted his hands, displaying the bandages on his fingers.

Wilkins gave a contemptuous grunt. "We'll see, won't we? In the meantime, you might as well take this." He snatched the cloth off the desk, then bundled it up and shoved it at Theo. "It's not like we can do anything else with it, and mayhap the sight of it'll remind you of what your incompetence is costing his nibs."

Privately, Theo doubted his brother-in-law would be overly burdened by the loss of two ells of cotton fabric. Still, he resisted the urge to regard Wilkins with the single lifted eyebrow which his late father had employed in dealing with impertinence, and instead took the bundle of cloth without a word. Far from being pleased with this display of restraint, however, Wilkins seemed almost disappointed not to have goaded Theo into some show of temper. "Now, get back to work," the foreman growled, clearly for lack of anything better to say.

"Yes—sir," Theo said, and suited the word to the deed.

Having nothing better to do with it, he stored the bundle of cloth with his basket of food, and when work was suspended at noon, he lost no time in seeking out Ben and taking a seat next to him at the long table.

"I see you've come prepared today," Ben remarked as Theo unpacked his basket.

"Yes," he admitted before continuing somewhat sheepishly, "I must thank you again for what you did for me yesterday. If you'd like to share my meal, you're welcome. I'm sure I couldn't eat the half of it," he added with perhaps less than perfect truth, as his stomach had rumbled in anticipation at the sight of the thick roast beef sandwich.

"That's all right. I've got my own." In proof of this, he unpacked his own midday meal, a rather sparser repast comprising a scrawny chicken leg and a boiled potato.

"So," Theo began in an offhand manner that, had he but known it, did not deceive the old man for a moment, "were you at the meeting last night?"

Ben's sparse gray eyebrows lifted, pushing into sharp relief the wrinkles that lined his forehead. "Oh, so you know about that, do you?"

"I could hardly help it! It was held in Mrs. Drinkard's dining room, which is situated directly below my bed-chamber. Ben, what's it all about?"

"What do you think?"

"I should say," Theo said thoughtfully, recalling the

snatches of conversation—if one could call it that—which had drifted up through the flue, "that Sir Valerian Wadsworth is trying to stir up unrest at the mill."

Old Ben inclined his head in a manner that reminded Theo forcefully of his old tutor congratulating him on correctly performing some difficult sum. "I think you're very likely right."

"But—but to what purpose?"

"What do you think?" Ben asked again.

"I wish you would stop answering my questions by asking me what I think!" Theo grumbled. "I should guess he's trying to stir up a riot, like those Luddites. But all that was years ago! Nothing like that happens now," he insisted, with all the certainty of a young man to whom the events of four years earlier might be considered ancient history.

"Mayhap you're right," conceded Ben. "But there will always be envious and discontented men, and when they're encouraged to band together and air their grievances—" he shrugged his stooped shoulders.

Time to take action . . . "If only airing grievances were all there was to it," Theo said, recalling the ominous words spoken in anger, and the other voices that had joined in, echoing their support. He lowered his voice still further, and asked urgently, "Shouldn't someone—I don't know—*do* something?"

Ben glanced to the far side of the room, where a phalanx of men huddled at the opposite end of the long table, whispering together. Abel Wilkins had now joined their number and, far from breaking up the little group, appeared to be listening to their conversation with interest. "And what do you suggest we do?"

"E—er, that is, Sir Ethan should be told, at the very least."

"He's in London, getting ready to stand for Parliament."

"Yes, but he needs to know, so he can put a stop to it," Theo insisted.

"Aye, mayhap he does, but what would you? Anyone who squeaks beef would have to answer to Abel there"—a nod toward Wilkins at the opposite end of the table—"and how to get word to Ethan anyway? We can hardly walk up to his house and knock on the door."

Perhaps you *can't,* thought Theo, setting his jaw, *but* I *can.*

* * *

His mind made up, Theo did not set out for Mrs. Drinkard's boardinghouse after his workday had ended, but turned off the main road as soon as possible—it would not do to be seen, by either the mill workers or the other residents of the boardinghouse, lest awkward questions be asked—and set out in the direction of his brother-in-law's house. Upon reaching this familiar residence, he rapped sharply upon the door with the polished brass knocker. A moment later the door opened to reveal Evers, the butler, who goggled upon recognizing the visitor.

"My lord Tisdale! That is, your grace!" he exclaimed, taking in every detail of Theo's changed appearance, from the sweat-soaked workman's smock to the bundle of cloth under his arm. "What—?"

"Shhh!" commanded Theo, glancing about to make certain the butler's involuntary exclamation had not been overheard. "Stubble it, will you?"

"Yes, your grace, er, sir," he amended hastily.

"I lost a wager," said Theo, seeking recourse to the explanation proposed by his brother-in-law. "Just keep it mum."

"Wild horses shall not drag it from my lips," promised Evers in failing accents. He had no very high opinion of the frequent demands of his mistress's relations upon his master's purse and, consequently, no desire to make known their latest misdeeds to the world—or, more specifically, to the household staffs of the neighboring gentry.

"The thing is, I've got to see Nell."

"I am sorry to disappoint you, your grace—er, sir," Evers said with perhaps less than perfect truth. "But Lady Helen is not at home."

"D'you mean she's absent, or that she isn't receiving visitors?" demanded Theo. "Because if it's the latter—"

He made as if to push his way into the house by main force, but Evers, having long experience in repelling unwanted callers, deftly prevented this move by the simple expedient of blocking the opening with his own rather stout person. "I regret to inform you that Lady Helen left for London yesterday morning."

"The devil she did! When does she plan to return?"

"She did not inform me, sir." Theo muttered an oath in response, and Evers, seeing his case was apparently urgent, decided to take pity on him. "I believe it is her intention to assist Sir Ethan in his Parliamentary bid. If I may take the liberty of speculating, I should think she will be absent for some weeks."

"Yes, I daresay you're right," Theo conceded, albeit grudgingly. "Thank you for telling me. I suppose I shall have to write, then. Can you get me into Ethan's study without anyone else seeing, do you think?"

"The rest of the staff is busy with dinner preparations," Evers informed him loftily. "If you will follow me, your grace?"

"Good man!" said Theo, following with furtive steps as the butler led the way across the hall to the room that served as his brother-in-law's study. Once inside, he closed the door against prying eyes and scrawled a hasty missive warning Ethan that something deuced havey-cavey was afoot at the mill, and urging him to come look into the matter. He signed it with a flourish, sealed it with a blob of wax dripped from the candle, and surrendered it to the butler, impressing upon Evers the need to post it to London by the next morning's mail.

"Meanwhile," he concluded, pausing on the front stoop to repeat these instructions as he took his leave, "not a word about my presence in the area!"

A sharp autumn breeze lifted the golden hair from his bare head, wafting in the butler's direction the odor of industry that clung to Theo's smock.

Evers shuddered. "I can assure you, your grace," he said, puckering his nostrils, "I shouldn't dream of it."

9

I belong to that highly respectable tribe
Which is known as the Shabby Genteel.
ANONYMOUS, "The Shabby Genteel," from *A Poor Relation*

As the following day was Sunday, Theo was granted a brief respite from the mill. The day brought its own challenges, however, as he was obliged to invent an excuse for not attending church with the other residents of the boardinghouse. Here he found an unexpected ally in Miss Drinkard, who urged him to take advantage of the opportunity to rest and recover from his unaccustomed labors, even going so far as to make his excuses to the rest of the party. In fact, this took no small degree of diplomacy, for Mr. Nutley was to give the sermon that day, as the vicar was ill, and the boardinghouse residents were loud in their expressions of eagerness to hear him undertake a responsibility which he was only rarely called upon to perform.

If Daphne had known what awaited her at church that day, however, it is quite possible that she would not have been so obliging; she had expressed a hope that she and Theo might be friends, and it soon transpired that she would need all the friends she could get. For among those present at divine services that morning was a rather dashing young matron rejoicing in the title of Lady Dandridge. Daphne had known this young woman as Kitty Morecombe; in fact, they were to have been presented in London during the same Season, had not the death of Daphne's father caused an abrupt and irrevocable change of plans.

"Daphne!" cried Lady Dandridge as soon as services were over and the final "amen" was said. "Daphne Drinkard, as I live and breathe!"

Squeezing past her husband in an attempt to exit her family's pew ahead of the departing worshippers, she hurried up to Daphne and seized her hands.

"How good it is to see you again! *Dandridge!*" she called, blonde ringlets bouncing as she turned to address her husband over her shoulder. "Dandridge, you must come and let me make you known to one of my oldest and dearest friends!"

They were joined at once by Lord Dandridge, a ruddy-faced and somewhat stocky gentleman of about thirty who had the look of a sportsman, and who would almost certainly grow stout in later years. "Eh? What's that, Kit?"

"Dandridge, my dear, this is Daphne Drinkard," said his fond spouse, blithely disregarding the unspoken rule decreeing that a gentleman should always be presented to a lady, rather than the other way 'round. "She and I were to have made our come-outs together, you know, but then her father died only weeks before we were to have gone to London. And how lucky for me that he did, for she always cast me quite into the shade at all the local assemblies, you know, and I daresay she would have done so in London as well. Why, you might have offered for her instead of for me!"

She pouted prettily at the very idea, and Lord Dandridge was quick to demur. "Not at all, Kit, my dear. Not that Miss Drinkard ain't a deuced pretty girl," he added quickly and with some alarm, as if he were unsure how to reassure one lady without insulting the other.

"But how well you look!" continued Kitty Dandridge, subjecting Daphne to an admiring scrutiny that somehow had the effect of making her all the more conscious of her three-year-old walking dress and the signs of wear on her kid gloves. "You know I've always thought that dress was particularly becoming on you. But you simply *must* add more flounces 'round the hem, you know! No one is wearing less than two these days, and very likely more. Why, I'm sure all my own gowns are trimmed from knee to ankle!"

As if in proof of this statement, she thrust out one small foot, pointing her toe in such a way as to call attention not only to her heavily ornamented hem, but also to the shapely, silk-clad ankle it concealed.

Daphne, still smarting over the assertion that her father's death might be considered a stroke of great good fortune, found herself quite incapable of admiring her old friend's fashionable clothing as Lady Dandridge obviously expected. Daphne had always marveled at, and perhaps secretly admired, her friend's ability to say the most outrageous things with so much vivacity and good humor that it was impossible to take offense. Now, for the first time, it occurred to her that Kitty's artless conversation was perhaps not so artless after all. Indeed, to lavish compliments that served only to demean their recipient was surely its own brand of cruelty.

"I'm—I'm glad things have worked out so well for you, Kitty," she said, and tried her best to mean it.

"But what of you? Surely you don't mean to remain here and become a dried-up old maid!"

I don't see that I have a great deal of choice in the matter, Daphne thought bitterly, but would never have admitted as much aloud, even had she been given the opportunity.

"You'll never meet any eligible gentlemen here," continued Lady Dandridge, casting a disdainful eye toward the door, beyond which a handful of locals could be seen lingering about the churchyard.

"On the contrary," Daphne protested, forcing a laugh she did not feel. "We've had a possible Member of Parliament visiting in the area, and—and there is a very handsome young man staying at the board—at the house—" She could not bring herself to call her family home a boardinghouse out loud, and within the hearing of one who might not be such a dear friend as Daphne had always believed. But she need not have worried, as Lady Dandridge would very likely have failed to notice in any case.

"A *Member of Parliament?* Oh Daphne, how wonderful if he should conceive a *tendre* for you!"

"You sound just like Mama! But he isn't a Member of Parliament yet, you know. He has to win a seat first."

"I shall have Dandridge make a donation to his

campaign," Kitty announced with the air of the Lady Bountiful. "Dandridge, you will see to it, won't you?"

It occurred to Daphne that Lord Dandridge might know something about the mysterious Mr. Tisdale. "But about this young man staying at the house," she began, turning to address his lordship, "I wonder, my lord, if you are acquainted with a gentleman by the name of—"

"Got a sudden notion," Lord Dandridge exclaimed, displaying a lack of attentiveness equal to anything his wife could offer. "No need for Miss Drinkard to remain here at all."

"What's that, my dear?" asked Kitty, lines of displeasure tightening about her mouth.

"Take her back to London with us. You'd like a companion, wouldn't you? She needs to see something of the world. There it is, then!" He rocked on the toes of his feet, clearly quite pleased with his own cleverness.

"Oh, my lord," breathed Daphne, overcome at the prospect opening up before her, "how very, *very* kind of you—"

"Dandridge, my dear, you cannot have thought," Kitty protested with a titter of laughter that held very little of humor. "Daphne doesn't have the right clothes for such a visit. We wouldn't want to embarrass her by having her come to us looking like a dowd!"

Even Lord Dandridge appeared somewhat taken aback by his wife's lack of tact. "Nonsense! What I mean is, no such thing. Couldn't look like a dowd if you tried," he assured Daphne with perhaps more diplomacy than truth.

"It's very kind of you to say so," Daphne told him

warmly, even as her hopes and dreams plummeted abruptly back down to earth. "And of course I should love to come and visit, but I'm afraid I can't leave my mother just at present."

"Yes, how is your poor mother?" Kitty asked, all eager sympathy now that she was no longer faced with the prospect of playing hostess to a shabby-genteel friend who might still contrive to cast her into the shade. "Pray excuse me, Daphne. I simply *must* say something to dear Mrs. Drinkard, for Dandridge and I return to London first thing in the morning, you know."

With these words, she flitted away, leaving Daphne alone with Lord Dandridge, who shuffled his feet awkwardly.

"Pay no heed to the things Kitty says. She don't mean half of 'em, you know."

"While as for the other half, she never stops to consider how they must sound to those on the receiving end," she concurred, nodding in understanding. "I assure you, my lord, I have known Kitty for a very long time—far too long to let her disconcerting remarks upset me."

And it was true, she told herself a short time later, as she accompanied her mother on the walk from the church to the boardinghouse. She had certainly known Kitty Morecombe too long, and too well, to be distressed by her verbal jabs. Furthermore, if Kitty had told the truth when she'd claimed to have been cast into the shade by Daphne (and whatever else might be said of her, Kitty was nothing if not brutally frank), well, perhaps one could not blame her for taking a certain satisfaction in the knowledge that she had made an advantageous marriage while the friend who had once outshone her was left to languish on the shelf.

Still, it was only with difficulty that Daphne held up her end of the conversation at nuncheon, most of which centered on praising Mr. Nutley for the excellence of his sermon. As soon as she could, she excused herself from the table, pausing only long enough to exchange her good Sunday walking dress for her faded blue muslin round gown before making her way down the neglected garden behind the house to the river that flowed some little distance away. She walked across the stone footbridge spanning the water until she reached the apex at its center, then braced her arms against the parapet and leaned over, gazing down at the waters rushing beneath her.

It was here, a short time later, that Theo found her. "Miss Drinkard? May I join you?"

She summoned a smile that was perhaps not quite so feeble as it might have been only a few minutes earlier. "Please do."

He stepped up onto the bridge and crossed it in half a dozen long, easy strides, pausing next to her at its highest point. "Forgive me, Miss Drinkard, but is anything wrong? I couldn't help noticing at nuncheon that you seemed to be troubled."

She looked up at him in some alarm. "You—you don't think Mama noticed, do you?"

He shook his head. "I doubt it. She, along with everyone else at the table, seemed far more interested in congratulating Mr. Nutley on his sermon." Thinking that she might be more inclined to confide in him if he could engage her first in some other topic of conversation, he asked, "Does it not seem to you that Mr. Nutley is rather old for a curate? I should have thought he would have a church of his own by this time."

"And so he might have had, were it not for a"—she lowered her voice, although there was no one else in sight—"an unfortunate incident in his youth."

"An 'unfortunate incident'?" echoed Theo, grinning broadly. "I can't imagine Mr. Nutley committing any indiscretion worthy of blighting a clerical career."

"Nor can I," Daphne confessed solemnly. "That's what makes it so sad."

Theo's smile faded in the face of her disinclination to laugh. "What happened, then?"

She hesitated for a moment, then said, "You must not let on that I told you, or that you know about it at all." Upon his agreeing to these conditions, she began. "As I said, he was very young at the time. He had just taken holy orders, and was invited to a dinner party at which the Archbishop of Canterbury was present, along with several other church leaders, any one of whom might have had the power to make his career."

"I should have thought that was a piece of rare good fortune," Theo observed.

"So it might have been, but I believe he used to be painfully shy when he was young, and was quite intimidated by the company in which he found himself. Dinner in those days was always served *à la française*, but poor Mr. Nutley was so afraid of saying something wrong that he dared not ask for any of the dishes farther up the table to be passed to him, and so terrified of dropping the heavy platter in front of him

SHERI COBB SOUTH

that he resolved not to pass it around the table unless he absolutely had to. Instead, he limited himself exclusively to the dish immediately before him."

"A dull meal," Theo remarked. "I hope he at least impressed the archbishop with his Christian humility."

"He might have done so," she conceded, "had the dish in question not been a platter of ruffs and reeves."

Theo let out a long, low whistle.

"Oh, you know what they are, then? I did not, until Mama told me."

"They're shore birds—male and female of the same species. I believe they are considered a delicacy."

"Yes, so Mama said. They were also," she said pointedly, "a particular favorite of the archbishop."

"Of course they were," Theo said in a flat voice.

"You can guess the result. A young man's very natural reluctance to put himself forward in such company was taken instead for gluttony, and selfishness, and pride, and just about every other vice one can imagine." She shrugged. "And that was the end of Mr. Nutley's clerical career. A family connection—an uncle, I believe, or some such relation—managed to procure for him a position as a curate, but from there he could rise no further. No letter of recommendation, whatever its source, had the power to overcome that disastrous first impression."

"But—but no one should have to suffer forever just because they did something stupid when they were young!" protested Theo, recalling with shame more than a few stupid actions of his own, committed not so very long ago and with far less cause.

"No," Daphne agreed sadly. "But what can one do?"

Theo, remembering several letters endorsing various curates for a vacant living which was within the Duke of Reddington's gift, thought that, however powerless Daphne and the other residents of the boardinghouse might be, he was in a position to do quite a bit. Aloud, he merely said, "I see I shall have to express my regrets to Mr. Nutley for having missed his sermon. I did so at nuncheon, of course, but it appears something more is in order. Should I say I'd heard it was—what? Comforting? Challenging? What the deuce does one say about a sermon, anyway?"

Daphne considered the matter. "Tell him you heard it was very thought-provoking," she suggested at last. In fact, she had not been able to concentrate on the sermon as the middle-aged curate deserved; she had been too aware of her old friend Kitty, now Lady Dandridge, seated in the box pew across the aisle with her fashionable new clothes and her aristocratic husband.

"I shall do so," Theo promised. "Now, having taken care of Mr. Nutley, let us turn our attention to you. I know your concern for Mr. Nutley is sincere, but I *don't* think that's what drove you from the house as soon as nuncheon was over."

"Oh, *that*," said Daphne, affecting a careless little laugh that didn't deceive Theo for a moment. "It is the stupidest thing, really. An old friend of mine was at church this morning, one whom I hadn't seen in several years. I knew her as Kitty Morecombe, only she is Lady Dandridge now, for she is married, and—oh, *bother!*" She broke off abruptly as hot tears blurred her vision.

"And you—you had hoped to marry Lord Dandridge yourself?" Theo asked, feeling suddenly as if someone had punched him in the stomach. He was a little acquainted with Lord Dandridge—a good enough sort, in his way, and an excellent fellow in the hunt. But not at all a proper husband for Daphne, although he could not have said exactly why this was so.

"No, of course not! That is, he seemed like a very amiable man—he even suggested that I might come to London and stay with them awhile."

"Well then, I think—I think you should go," Theo said, all the while selfishly hoping the proposed visit would not take place until after he was free to leave the boardinghouse.

"So I might have done, but Kitty pointed out that I haven't any proper clothes for such a visit, and—and would only look like a dowd."

"Well, I'm dashed!" Theo exclaimed indignantly. "Of all the rag-mannered—"

"She was quite right," Daphne put in quickly. "I *don't* have any proper clothes, and I would not want to embarrass them. I know they couldn't have sponsored me for the Season or anything of that nature, but it would have been rather nice to see St. Paul's, or go to the theatre, or watch the equestrian performers at Astley's Amphitheatre."

"You wouldn't have liked Astley's at all," Theo assured her with, perhaps, less than perfect truth. "You'd no doubt have found yourself rubbing shoulders with a bunch of mushrooms."

She regarded him with some amusement. "It may have escaped your notice, Mr. Tisdale, but I *am* a mushroom."

He could only stare at her. Was she serious? Any fool with eyes in his head could see that Miss Drinkard was a lady! And yet, he remembered his first night at the boardinghouse, and his sentiments upon sitting down to dinner with, as he had thought of them, a bunch of shabby-genteel mushrooms. "I— I like mushrooms," he found himself saying.

"I beg your pardon?"

"I like mushrooms," he said again, with more conviction in his voice. "Especially if they're cooked in a wine sauce and served over chicken. Without them, it's just a bird, but with the mushrooms—well, let's just say that if they'd been an option at Mr. Nutley's dinner party, the archbishop would have forgotten all about those deuced ruffs and reeves."

This won a reluctant smile from Daphne, and so Theo was inspired to enlarge upon this theme. She did not believe him for one minute, of course. Still, she was glad he had not attempted to placate her with false assurances that she was not a mushroom. No, *I like mushrooms*, he'd said, and suddenly a mushroom had seemed a very excellent thing to be.

That night, alone in her tiny bedchamber, she took out the writing pad she kept tucked away beneath her mattress and began to write:

I know a lad with golden hair,
And leaf-green eyes, and courtly air . . .

The meter was simplistic, and the imagery was far from profound. Still, it contained a joy and an optimism that her poetry had not possessed for a very long time.

10

The tenderest love requires to be renewed by intervals of absence.
SAMUEL JOHNSON, *The Idler*

A cold autumn rain fell in sheets as the cumbersome traveling chaise containing Lady Helen Brundy and the younger of her twin sons lurched to a stop before the Grosvenor Square town house. The footman, who had been stationed in the foyer for the past two hours so as to be prepared for this vehicle's arrival, now stepped out onto the portico, unfurled his umbrella, and approached the carriage. He would have opened the door upon the two passengers, but his master, who had been awaiting the arrival of the chaise (or, rather, its occupants) far more impatiently, ran past him, heedless of his own lack of umbrella, hat, or any other protection from the inclement weather save for a caped greatcoat of dark twill. Sir Ethan wrenched the door open and beheld, for the first time in more than two weeks, his wife and child.

Neither had improved during the interim. The green of

Lady Helen's eyes stood out in stark relief against the dark circles beneath them, and although she was swathed in a thick pelisse, he rather thought she had lost weight; certainly, the face framed by its fashionable poke bonnet appeared somewhat thinner than he remembered. But far more striking than his wife's changed appearance was the deterioration in his son. Master William Brundy, familiarly known as Willie, sat on his mother's lap, where he had obviously been sleeping, at least until the cessation of the carriage's movement had awakened him. At age three, he had not yet lost his baby fat, but his plump cheeks were flushed an unnatural red, and his brown eyes, usually bright with mischief, were now dull.

"Willie?" Sir Ethan called softly to him.

"Papa," Willie moaned miserably, holding out his arms to his father.

Sir Ethan received him willingly, and tucked him within the folds of his greatcoat before holding out his free hand to his wife.

"Oh, Ethan, you're a sight for sore eyes," she said, sighing with the relief of a woman whose heart has come home. "Yes, I shall be only too happy to leave the carriage, but don't you think you should move aside so Matthew may lower the step? Take Willie into the house, and I shall be there directly."

Sir Ethan was much inclined to linger at her side, but Willie's appearance was enough to convince him that she was probably right. He gave Matthew a nod that was half instruction and half apology, then carried his son into the house, crooning assurances to the boy that Papa was here, and would very soon set everything to rights.

He only wished he could believe it.

Lady Helen entered the house a moment later, sheltering beneath Matthew's umbrella and clinging to his arm; alas, Willie's weight on her right leg had all but cut off the circulation of blood, and that usually reliable limb could no longer support her weight. Once inside, she removed her pelisse, and Sir Ethan's suspicions that she had lost weight were confirmed.

"You're looking well, Ethan," she observed with mingled envy and resentment. How very like a man to go haring off to London, leaving the women of his household to cope with the illness of one child and the clinginess of the three healthy ones, all of whom felt their sibling was claiming more than his fair share of maternal attention. Even as her brain formed the thought, she recognized the unfairness of the charge, and dismissed it without regret. "Yes, Willie, I know you want to stay with Papa, but at least allow him to remove his wet coat!"

With some reluctance, Willie abandoned the shelter of his father's arms for the mother with whom he had been shut up in a carriage for the better part of two days. Once this garment, along with Lady Helen's pelisse and bonnet, had been surrendered to Matthew and whisked away to dry before the fire, Sir Ethan addressed himself to his wife. "So you think I look well, do you? I wish I could say the same for you! You look worn to the bone, love."

"I am. But how very unhandsome of you to say so!"

Sir Ethan offered no answer to this charge, but shifted

Willie to one arm so that he might enfold his wife in the other. "But I thought you were going to stay in Lancashire until he was better."

"I was," she said, fighting an uncharacteristic urge to burst into tears on her husband's shoulder. "But he didn't seem to be getting any better, and finally I thought it might be best to bring him with me, so a doctor might see him."

"There are doctors in Lancashire," he pointed out.

These rural practitioners of the medical arts, however, found no favor with Lady Helen, who made a noise which, in a less elegant female, might have been called a snort. "Yes! Old Dr. Forrest, who would no doubt wish to bleed him and dose him with laudanum!" In a more moderate tone, she added, "Perhaps I should have waited, but I had no idea we would be arriving in the worst possible weather for an invalid; it was perfectly fine when we left Lancashire! Then, too, I thought perhaps removing Willie from their sphere might at least keep the other children from falling ill. And I wanted to see you again. I've missed you, Ethan."

There was only one possible response to this confession. He tightened his arm about her and kissed her lingeringly, chuckling a little when Willie's plump arm released his neck in order to wrap itself around hers, uniting them in a circle of three.

"Oh, it is good to be here," Lady Helen said with another sigh, this time one of contentment. "I confess, just as the children look to me to make everything right, even when there is nothing I can do, I look to you."

"Even when there's nothing I can do?" he murmured

against the honey-colored hair tickling his nose.

"Even when," she agreed, and reluctantly detached herself from his embrace. "But I must go upstairs to the nursery and get Willie into bed. Will you come with me?"

"You just try and stop me," he said, and together they climbed the two flights of stairs to the nursery.

The children spent most of their time in Lancashire, but one of the rooms below the eaves had been fitted out as a nursery for those occasions when their parents chose to bring them to Town. The girl who had been pressed into service as a temporary nursery maid had done her job well, for a fire already burned in the grate, and a lump beneath the sheets of Willie's narrow bed suggested the presence of a hot brick. Nor had Matthew, the footman, been idle since their arrival, for Willie's bag had been brought up to the nursery, and the maid had unpacked his clothes and spread his nightshirt across the back of a chair positioned before the fire.

"I know I should have laid it out on the bed, your ladyship," the nursery maid offered apologetically, seeing her mistress's gaze falling upon this last. "But I thought as how it might best be warmed, it being so cold and wet outside, and Matthew telling us all downstairs as how sick the poor mite was."

"No, you did very well," Lady Helen assured her warmly. "It was clever of you to think of it."

The girl, fairly beaming at this praise, was all eagerness to earn more. "Shall I fetch up some broth? There'll be some in the kitchen, I know, for Cook was boiling a chicken for a fricassee."

Lady Helen glanced at her son. Willie's head now drooped upon his father's shoulder, and he knuckled his eyes with one small fist. "Not yet," she said. "He must sleep for now, but he will certainly want broth when he awakens. You need not stay; I shall put him to bed myself."

"Yes ma'am," said the maid, bobbing a curtsey before betaking herself from the room.

Lady Helen sat on the edge of the bed and soon had young Master William stripped, gowned, and tucked between warm sheets. "Sleep well, my pet," she whispered, and bent to kiss the dark curls that were so like his father's.

Once they had left the nursery and closed the door softly behind them, Sir Ethan bent a critical eye on his wife. "And now, love, I think it's your turn."

"My turn for what?"

"Your turn to be coddled. It's plain as a pikestaff you've worn yourself out caring for Willie—and don't tell me the others 'aven't demanded their share of your attention, for I won't believe you."

"Well, no," she admitted. "I won't."

"So now it's time someone took care of you," he continued. "I'm going to put you to bed and see that you sleep 'til next Tuesday."

She gave a half-hearted laugh. "Don't tempt me! But it was to help with your Parliamentary bid that I promised to join you in London. I daresay we shall be obliged to attend a great many dinners, and I have no objection to hosting a few, but if you expect me to offer kisses in exchange for votes, as the Duchess of Devonshire did—"

"If that's what it takes to win, I'd just as soon lose," put in Sir Ethan, steering her into the bedchamber.

"Then too, I should like to look in on Teddy," she continued. "I daresay he is going on well enough—at least, I haven't heard anything to the contrary—but I should rest a great deal easier after seeing for myself."

"Oh, er, as to that," Sir Ethan hedged, seeing the hour of reckoning was at hand, " 'e's—'e's not in Town anymore."

"Has he taken up residence at Reddington Hall?" she asked in some surprise. "I trust nothing is wrong there?"

He hastened to reassure her. "Oh, no! Everything is fine"—the slightest pause—"there."

Alas, she was far too quick for his peace of mind. "And by that cryptic utterance, am I to understand that everything is *not* fine *here?*"

"It's not as bad as all that," was his not very reassuring reply. " 'e's just gone to Lancashire for awhile."

"To—oh, and I missed him! I daresay we must have passed one another upon the road. Still, I suppose the housekeeper will know what bedroom to give him, and I shall write with instructions for—"

" 'old up, 'elen," he said, raising a hand to forestall her. "There's no need for you to write the 'ousekeeper, for 'e'll not be staying at our 'ouse."

"Not—then where, pray, is he staying? He has no other acquaintances in the area, at least not to my knowledge."

" 'e'll 'ave plenty of acquaintances by now," he predicted grimly.

"Ethan," she said, regarding her spouse with a kindling

eye, "what have you done?"

"Me?" He gave her a look of wounded innocence. "What makes you think I've done anything?"

"If you haven't *done* anything, you certainly *know* something," she said with all the certainty of four years of marriage. "What, pray, is Teddy doing in Lancashire?"

"If you must know, 'e's working at the mill."

"He's *what?*"

"Shhh!" He put a finger to his lips. "We don't want to wake Willie."

"At the moment, Willie is the least of my concerns! Ethan, what has been happening here, and what have you done to my brother?"

"I just told you—"

Lady Helen took a deep breath. "Tell me the whole story from the beginning! *Why* is my brother working at the mill?"

"That's not the beginning. It's what you might call the middle."

Lady Helen strove with herself. "I have a feeling that is the very *last* of all the things I might call it! From the beginning, if you will be so kind!"

Now it was Sir Ethan's turn to take a deep breath. "Well, by the time your father's solicitor, and steward, and everyone else was done telling 'im what 'e'd 'ave to do as Duke, and 'ow unsuited to it 'e was—" He broke off abruptly and gestured toward the delicate Sheraton chair before her rosewood writing desk. "Per'aps you'd better sit down."

"I shall do very well standing," she said through clenched teeth.

"Aye, well—as I said, by the time they were all done with 'im, your brother was in a regular pucker, thinking as 'ow 'e wasn't fit to *fetch* 'is father's shoes, much less fill 'em. 'e lost 'is way for a time. Oh, 'e'll be all right, but in the meantime, 'e managed to spend, or lose, more money than 'e can pay until probate is granted."

Lady Helen's eyes widened in dawning comprehension. "Ethan! Is that what it was all about—La Fantasia, and all the rest?"

"Aye, love, that's what. La Fantasia was after 'im to marry 'er, and 'e felt played for a fool."

"Thank God he saw past her wiles! Papa would be spinning in his grave—as would every Duke of Reddington who'd come before him!"

"Your brother 'as more sense than that, and more recognition of what's due 'is name. Although," he added, "it's a wonder, what with your father treating 'im like a simpleton and you acting like 'e's still in leading strings."

"I never—!" Her husband regarded her with raised eyebrows, and she was obliged to amend her instinctive denial. "I suppose it's true that I've always been a little protective of Teddy, especially after Mama died. Papa's tongue-lashings can be brutal, you know."

"Can they?" Sir Ethan asked with interest, having been on the receiving end of his grace's temper on more than one occasion. "I'd never noticed."

"No, for they always rolled off you like water off a duck's back," she recalled with a trace of envy. "But then, you were never dependent upon him. I can assure you, for his children it was quite different! It would have been better for Teddy if he'd stood up to Papa."

He regarded her skeptically. "Would it really?"

"Yes," she insisted. "Oh, it wouldn't have changed anything—Papa would never have given in! But instead of defending himself, Teddy just—just withdrew."

"There's nothing wrong with walking away from a fight, 'elen," Sir Ethan pointed out reasonably. "Especially when you know you can't win. Sometimes the one 'oo walks away is the stronger man."

"Perhaps you're right," she conceded, considering her young brother in this new light. "But Papa always took his passivity as a sign of weakness. When we were young, he used to say that it was a great pity I was not a boy."

"I'll 'ave to disagree with 'im there," put in Sir Ethan.

Lady Helen gave him a speaking look, but refused to take the bait. "I own, I felt flattered at the time, although I never had the slightest desire to inherit the title. Looking back, though, I can't even imagine how it must have made Teddy feel."

"*I* can," Sir Ethan said darkly.

"Well, yes, I suppose I can, at that. But you say he ran up debts. You paid them, I gather."

"Aye, but only as a loan."

"Which, I take it, he'll pay back as soon as the will is probated," she surmised.

"No. 'e'll pay it back by working at the mill."

"Oh yes, this is where we started, isn't it? Ethan, you can't put a duke to work in a cotton mill!"

"I don't like to brangle with you, love, but I just did."

"What can you possibly hope to accomplish, besides utterly humiliating him?" She raised a hand to forestall his answer. "And don't speak to me of loans, for I know very well that no mill worker would earn the kind of money that Teddy could lose at White's in an evening, not if he were to work in the mill for a hundred years!"

"Per'aps 'e'll learn just that," Sir Ethan said. "Per'aps 'e'll value 'is in'eritance more once 'e sees for 'imself 'ow other men live. And while 'e's about it, per'aps 'e'll discover that 'e can do things 'e never thought 'e could, and that 'e's not quite the fool 'is father always took 'im for."

She considered this for a long moment. "Perhaps," she conceded, although her tone did not sound optimistic. "I only hope you know what you're doing. For my part, I still think he needs a wife."

"Aye, well, maybe 'e'll find one of them, too. Now," he said in a very different voice, "are you going to 'ave a lie-down and rest before dinner, or am I going to 'ave to strip you and put you to bed myself?"

She turned away as if to rebuff this suggestion, but cast a coy glance at him over her shoulder. "I should like to see you try!"

Sir Ethan, nothing loth, accepted this challenge with alacrity.

* * *

Not until after dinner did Sir Ethan turn his attention from family concerns to the business that had brought him to London in the first place.

"I've promised to meet Sir Lawrence Latham at Brooks's tonight," he informed his wife with a marked lack of enthusiasm. "I didn't know at the time that you'd be 'ere, love. I can cancel, if you like."

"You need not do so on my account," she assured him, looking up from the note that had been brought to the table along with the sweet course. "The doctor's wife says he has been called out to attend what may well be a deathbed, and cannot see William until tomorrow morning at the earliest. I confess, I am not entirely sorry. Now that the poor lamb is sleeping soundly, I should be extremely reluctant to wake him, even for the doctor to examine him. So you may leave him with a clear conscience."

"It wasn't Willie I was thinking of."

She laid aside her serviette and rose from the table. "You may leave me with a clear conscience, too. I intend to go to bed early and sleep until noon."

"And so you shall," he promised her. "If the doctor should 'appen to call while you're still abed, I'll take 'im up to Willie meself. You need not get up at all."

She gave a wistful sigh. "It's tempting, but he would think me a very unnatural parent. Go to your meeting, darling. I shall catch up on lost sleep, and see you after you return."

With this Sir Ethan was forced to be content, and yet he could not be entirely easy in his mind. He knew what he wanted—and wanted very badly, at that—but he also knew what he must do. And so it was that, upon his reaching Brooks's and being shown into the small private room where waited those bastions of the Whig party, Sir Lawrence Latham and Lord Grey, he bided his time only long enough for handshakes to be exchanged all around before declaring, "Gentlemen, I think I'd best drop out of the race."

His audience stared at him slack-jawed for a long moment before Sir Lawrence protested, "Drop out of the— damn it, man, you can't do this!"

"We've been laying the groundwork for your Parliamentary bid for months," pointed out Lord Grey. "Why would you choose to drop out now?"

"It's not a good time," Sir Ethan said. "Things 'ave changed since you first approached me. Me father-in-law 'as died, so me wife is in mourning, and I'm the executor of 'is will, so young Tisdale—the new Duke of Reddington, I should say—needs me. Then, too, me boy Willie is ill."

"I'm sorry for it, Brundy, truly I am," Lord Grey said in conciliatory tones. He sank into an upholstered armchair before the fire and gestured for the other men to do likewise. "But you must see—"

"Who would we find on such short notice to take your place?" demanded Sir Lawrence, all but bouncing on the edge of his seat in vexation. "Tell me that, if you can!"

"Your opponent has a powerful patron with deep pockets," continued Lord Grey, ignoring the interruption. "Sir Valerian Wadsworth's mother is the sister of the Earl of Mountlake. The earl is willing to shell out considerably to establish his nephew."

"I should've thought 'e was 'established' already," objected Sir Ethan. " 'im 'aving a title and all."

"Unfortunately, Sir Valerian's estate was depleted long

before he came into his inheritance. Since he left Oxford, he appears to have done little enough to restore it. In fact, it appears the fellow hasn't done much with himself at all, beyond leading a fashionably extravagant life in London, mostly at his uncle's expense."

"If 'e's as worthless as you say, 'e sounds as if 'e'd be an easy man to beat," Sir Ethan pointed out. "Almost anyone could stand against 'im and win."

"One might think so," conceded Lord Grey, "but then, one would be reckoning without the influence of his uncle. Mountlake appears determined to put an end to his nephew's continued feeding at the family trough, so to speak. He's investing a great deal in Sir Valerian's campaign, in terms of both money and influence."

"I understand your position, and I'm sorry for it," said Sir Ethan apologetically. "Per'aps next time—"

"If Sir Valerian is allowed to win the seat at this juncture, there'll be no booting him out of it later," Sir Lawrence predicted grimly.

"Alas, too true," seconded Lord Grey. "He may appear to be a worthless fribble, but Sir Valerian is not without a ruthless streak. If we're ever to have a trustworthy man in that position, Sir Valerian's political career must be nipped now, while it is still in the bud."

"Then, too, your withdrawal at this point would be perceived as unsteadiness of character," Sir Lawrence continued. "It would be held against you, should you decide to stand in some future election."

Sir Ethan put forward every argument he could muster—

and these were many—but Lord Grey, or Sir Lawrence, or both had an answer for them all. Had he really done his best to wriggle out of it, he wondered, or had he allowed himself to be persuaded because it was what he wanted all along?

He was still wrestling with this home question when he returned to Grosvenor Square. The house was dark; apparently his wife had not lied when she'd said she intended to seek her bed early. He let himself into the house with his own key, and glanced idly at the little pile of letters lying on a silver tray on a table beside the door. Lady Helen had evidently retired even before the late post had been delivered. He picked up the letters and carried them into his study, where a fire had been lit in anticipation of his return. He shuffled through the stack of correspondence: three or four invitations, most of which must be declined due to his wife's bereaved state; one letter to his wife from Emily, Lady Cutliffe, which could wait until morning; a couple of bills, forwarded from Lancashire, from suppliers for raw materials for the mill, and—

He recognized the handwriting on the outside of the single sheet, and muttered under his breath something that would certainly have got Willie's mouth washed out with soap. Sir Ethan sighed. At the moment, he had a sick child and a wife worn out with nursing, a deceased father-in-law who had saddled him with the responsibility of serving as his executor, a Parliamentary bid that might well be over even before it began, and a young brother-in-law who showed every sign of repeating the wastrel proclivities of generations of Dukes of Reddington before him. The last thing he needed at the moment was a message from that same brother-in-law bemoaning his present condition and begging for a reprieve.

"You young fool," Sir Ethan grumbled, albeit not without affection, for he was genuinely fond of Theo. "Don't you see I'm giving you your last, best chance?"

Hardening his heart, he tossed the letter, unopened, into the fire.

11

All's fair in love and war.
FRANCIS EDWARD SMEDLEY, *Frank Fairlegh*

Daphne stood in the middle of the footbridge spanning the river that flowed some little distance behind the house, idly plucking petals from the last of the late-blooming wildflowers and dropping them one by one into the swirling waters beneath her feet. She should, she knew, be in the kitchen helping Cook with the dinner preparations, but the prospect of a few moments of privacy (an unaccustomed luxury when one's home was turned into a boardinghouse) had proven impossible to resist. Then, too, there was the fact that Mr. Tisdale would soon be returning from the mill. In the fortnight since he had taken up residence in the house, Daphne had become all too aware that her ear was now attuned to the sound of his footsteps in the hall, his weary tread as he climbed the stairs to his room.

Her brow furrowed at the thought of this last. It was obvious that he was not accustomed to the work. She wished she might do something to relieve his burden—something beyond the bandaging of his poor blistered hands. But when she cast about in her mind for some new form of relief, the only ideas that presented themselves were sufficient to bring the blood rushing to her face. It would not do, this undue concern for Mr. Tisdale's well-being. He seemed to think that his financial difficulties were temporary; she must hope, against her own inclinations, that he was correct, for it would be a very poor friend who would rejoice in the hardships of another merely so that she might continue to enjoy his company. And yet, there was no denying the fact that with his departure, her days would be all the bleaker for having been given that brief glimpse of sunshine.

Heaving a sigh, she tossed the denuded stem into the water. The days were growing shorter with the retreat of summer, and the light was now fading. Her mother would be wondering what had become of her. It would not do for Mama to suspect that her daughter was given to daydreaming about a mill worker, no matter how genteel his manners.

"Miss Drinkard?"

Upon hearing herself hailed by a masculine voice, her heart gave a great leap, only to settle, upon discovering that the speaker was in fact not Mr. Tisdale, but Sir Valerian Wadsworth, somewhere in the region usually occupied by her stomach.

"Sir Valerian!" she exclaimed, trying to sound pleased. "How you startled me!"

"Did I? In that case, I must beg your pardon."

"I'm sure there is no need for you to apologize," Daphne protested. "If I was startled, I have no one but myself to blame, for I fear I was woolgathering. It is not often that I find time alone to think. Not, of course, that it isn't always a pleasure to see you," she added lamely, realizing that this last observation was hardly flattering to her present company. To be sure, Mama expected her to do all she could to attach Sir Valerian's interest, but she could not be easy in his presence or, if the truth be known, even like him very much. This was, perhaps, a little unfair, as he had given her no reason to hold him in dislike. No reason, at least, beyond the fact that he was not Mr. Tisdale.

But Sir Valerian proved impervious to insult. In fact, far from being offended, he seemed to find her preoccupation amusing. "Were you woolgathering indeed? Now, what might a young lady find to occupy her thoughts to such a degree, but a young man? Dare I hope to be the one? Aha! The flags flying in her cheeks give me hope!"

Daphne was indeed blushing crimson, but Sir Valerian was quite mistaken as to the source of her embarrassment. It was not that she had been dreaming of Sir Valerian, but the fact that she should have been, and yet was not, that caused her such distress. She could hardly point out his error, however, so she made as if to return to the house.

"If you will excuse me, sir, I must go. Mama will be expecting me to help her and Cook with the dinner preparations."

Far from stepping aside to let her pass, he took a step closer and caught one of her hands in his. "Very well, Miss Drinkard, I shan't tease you. Only allow me to say that I consider it a great pity that these small hands should bear so heavy a burden."

"By all means you may say so, Sir Valerian," she said crisply, snatching her hand away, "if *you* will allow *me* to say that I consider it a great pity that a man of your exalted stature should choose to express himself in terms better suited to an actor in a Christmas pantomime."

With this home thrust, she brushed past him and hurried up the path to the house.

"*There* you are!" exclaimed Mrs. Drinkard as Daphne entered the house through the back door that opened onto the kitchen. "Here's Cook needing someone to shell peas, and you nowhere in sight!"

"I beg your pardon, Mama. I had not meant to neglect my chores. It is only that I was down by the river, talking to Sir Valerian."

At this revelation, Mrs. Drinkard's ill humor evaporated, as Daphne had known it would. "Oh, my dear! If only you might attach his interest, all our difficulties would be at an end! What a good thing you had not yet put on your old gown! But you must do so now, for Cook has need of you."

"Yes, Mama, I shall do so at once. Only—tell me, what brought Sir Valerian here?"

"He said he wanted to speak to me regarding my permission—well, you may guess what I thought of *that!*"

"Your—your permission?"

Mrs. Drinkard gave a huff of annoyance. "My permission to hold another of his abominable meetings! Only fancy— here I was, thinking he was about to request my permission to pay his addresses to you, my love, and all he wanted was to fill my dining room with those odious mill workers again!"

"Oh," Daphne said, secretly relieved. "I suppose the first meeting must have gone very well, then."

"Apparently," her mother agreed without enthusiasm. "Still, I suppose it keeps him in the neighborhood, so . . ." She dismissed the thought with a shrug, which Daphne took as her signal.

"If you will excuse me, Mama, I'll change into an old gown and be down to help Cook in a trice."

Suiting the word to the deed, she left the kitchen for the more public part of the house. She hurried up the stairs (noting once more the signs of wear on the carpet that covered the treads) and started down the corridor toward her own room. Before she reached it, however, the door to Mr. Potts's bedchamber flew open and the aspiring lawyer stepped into the corridor.

"Miss Drinkard," he addressed her somewhat stiffly, "I have been awaiting your return."

"Have you?" she asked in some confusion. She glanced toward the open door behind him. "Is something amiss with your lodgings? Do you require fresh towels, perhaps?"

He made an impatient gesture of dismissal. "Towels be hanged! My window overlooks the back of the house, you know. I saw you with Sir Valerian."

She sighed, having a very fair idea of the direction the conversation was about to take. "Yes? What of it?"

"Miss Drinkard, I must caution you against encouraging that man's advances. I fear his intentions toward you cannot be honorable."

"I was not aware that you were so well acquainted with Sir Valerian," she said coolly, wondering why every gentleman of her acquaintance suddenly seemed determined to address her in terms usually heard only on the stage.

"I'm not." Mr. Potts made this declaration as if it were a source of considerable pride.

"Then what, pray, can you know of his intentions?"

"Permit me to observe, Miss Drinkard, that I know rather more of the world than you have had occasion to learn. I have attended Oxford, you know, and before taking up my present position, I was accustomed to spending the summers with my aunt in Yorkshire, where I attended both the cathedral and the assemblies."

"Yorkshire," echoed Daphne. "How very cosmopolitan!"

"Don't laugh at me!" Mr. Potts ground out through clenched teeth. "You must know how I feel about you!"

"Indeed, I could not fail to do so, Mr. Potts, although I am sure I have never given you the least encouragement! I fear I can give you no hope, and can only urge you to fix your interests on some other, more receptive object."

"Never!" declared Mr. Potts. Before she realized what he was about, he had seized her in his arms. "I shall never love anyone but you!"

"Stop it! Mr. Potts, you must not! Release me this minute, before I box your ears!"

In fact, this was an empty threat, as her arms were pinned to her sides. In any case, he paid her not the slightest heed, but attempted to capture her mouth with his own—an assault which Daphne could only resist (and that with only mixed success) by twisting her head from side to side. Above their labored breathing, she was vaguely aware of muffled footsteps on the stairs—a familiar tread that increased rapidly once it reached the uncarpeted corridor. In the next instant, Mr. Potts let out a strangled cry as his cravat tightened about his neck like a noose and he was hauled backwards by his collar. He perforce released Daphne, who, although flushed and breathing heavily, nevertheless looked beyond his shoulder to regard her deliverer with glowing eyes.

"You will make your apologies to Miss Drinkard at once," commanded Theo, giving his captive a shake as a terrier might a rat.

Mr. Potts glared at Theo over his shoulder as much as the viselike grip on his collar would allow. "And why should I take orders from a common laborer?"

"Because if you don't, this common laborer is going to take you outside and give you the thrashing you deserve."

Although a stranger to Yorkshire, Theo stood fully half a head taller than his vanquished foe and had more than once boxed with Gentleman Jackson in the former champion's Bond Street saloon. Although Mr. Potts had no way of knowing of the latter circumstance, he was all too aware of the former. Whatever his shortcomings as a lover, he had not progressed so far in his chosen profession by being stupid, and he quickly reached the conclusion that here was one of those instances where discretion was indeed the better part of valor.

"Very well," the fledgling lawyer said stiffly. With these words, he found himself released so abruptly that he was hard-pressed not to stumble into the wall. Straightening himself to his full (albeit unimpressive) height, he tugged his disarranged clothing back into some semblance of order, and addressed Daphne with what dignity he could muster. "I am sorry if the ardor I have so long felt for you has betrayed me into giving offense. Believe me when I say I never would have insulted you with my attentions, had I the slightest notion that you preferred the lecherous advances of a London park-saunterer to the love of an honest man."

"Mr. Potts, you do both Sir Valerian and me an injustice—"

Ignoring her half-formed protest, the offended lawyer turned his disdain upon Theo. "As for you, I regret that the difference in our respective stations prohibits me from demanding satisfaction from you on the field of honor. Nevertheless, I will not spend one more night beneath the same roof as one I can only consider a ruffian and a bully-boy. Miss Drinkard, I shall settle my account with your mother, and then this house shall see me no more."

"Really, Mr. Potts, there is not the slightest need for you to—"

He paid her no heed, but ducked back into his room and slammed the door. Daphne and Theo regarded one another in silence for a long moment.

"Oh, dear," Daphne said at last, letting out a long breath.

"Are you all right?" Theo asked, regarding her keenly.

"Yes. That is, I'm not looking forward to breaking the news to Mama that she is losing one of her boarders, but other than that—" she broke off, shrugging.

"Surely your mother cannot expect you to tolerate such treatment, no matter how much income he brings!"

"No, indeed! And as much as I regret the manner of his leaving, I cannot deny it will make my life a great deal more comfortable. He seems to regard me as his personal property, and although I don't wish to hurt him, none of my attempts to hint him away have had the slightest effect!"

"Any man who can ignore 'release me before I box your ears' is incapable of being moved by hints," Theo assured her. "But—at the risk of seeming impertinent, I must ask: what do you really know of Sir Valerian?"

"I know that he is standing for Parliament, of course, and that he has been painstakingly honest in his dealings with Mama, for he has paid her in advance for the use of the dining room for his meetings. Oh, are you thinking of what Mr. Potts said about 'lecherous advances? It was nothing of the kind! He merely took my hand and—and tried to flirt with me. The merest nothing, really." All the same, Daphne felt her face grow warm at the memory.

"But you said 'meetings,' in the plural. Is he holding another one, then?"

"Yes," she said, fighting back a wholly irrational annoyance that he should find this information more compelling than the possibility that Sir Valerian might have been making unseemly advances to her. "Tomorrow night. Why? Do you want to attend?"

"I—I don't know. Perhaps I should."

Her fine dark eyes widened. "There's nothing wrong with them, is there?"

"I don't know," he said again. "I only know that there seems to be some sort of—I suppose you could call it unrest— at the mill. I should hate for you and your mother to find yourselves in the middle of some unpleasantness."

"Should I warn Mama, do you think? Perhaps she ought not to let him hold his meetings here."

"Say nothing to your mother, at least for the nonce. It may prove to be a storm in a teacup. I can hear something of the proceedings through the chimney flue. Perhaps after tomorrow night I shall have a better idea of what's going on."

"Or you could just attend the meeting yourself," she pointed out reasonably. "After all, they are for the mill workers—and you're a mill worker."

"Yes," he said thoughtfully, "but until I have a better idea of their purpose, I'm reluctant to align myself with them."

At that moment, a door opened at Theo's end of the corridor, and a moment later old Mr. Nethercote emerged from his bedchamber, dressed for dinner in all the finery of a quarter-century earlier.

"Oh!" Daphne exclaimed. "Mama will be expecting me to help Cook, and I haven't even changed my dress!"

"You may tell her it's my fault, for keeping you chatting in the corridor," Theo said gallantly.

And of all the excuses she might make, Daphne thought, that was the last one she would choose. Mama might excuse her dallying with Sir Valerian by the river, but lingering in the corridor to converse with, as Mr. Potts had said, a common laborer? Impossible. And on the subject of Mr. Potts . . .

"No matter how tardy I might be as a result, Mr. Tisdale,

I cannot go without first thanking you for coming to my aid," she said warmly, raising shining eyes to his. "I shall never forget it as long as I—" Suddenly conscious that she was saying too much, she broke off abruptly and ducked into her room quite as quickly as Mr. Potts had done.

She hastily divested herself of her second-best morning gown, donning instead a faded round gown of blue calico before hurrying down the stairs and through the baize door that led to the kitchens, as eager to avoid her mother's censure as she was to escape the realization that, had it been Mr. Tisdale who had seized her in his arms and covered her face with kisses, her response might have been quite different.

* * *

"Daphne, my love, you have miscounted," her mother chided, looking up from her own task of slicing bread to nod at the stack of plates Daphne carried. "You're a plate short. Now, what can be the cause of this sudden absentmindedness, I wonder?"

Her mother's coy manner and knowing look gave Daphne to understand that she was more than forgiven for her tardiness, so long as it was Sir Valerian who had been the cause of it. "There is no error in the number of plates, Mama. I—I believe Mr. Potts will not be dining with us." In fact, she had hoped that Mr. Potts had broken the news to her mother while she had been changing her dress. Her heart sank at the realization that this task must fall to her. She recalled hearing the sounds of heavy footsteps on the stairs as she dressed, followed by the slamming of the front door, and only hoped Mr. Potts had remembered to settle his account, as he had promised.

"Oh?" Mrs. Drinkard asked. "Why not? Surely he is not ill! Perhaps a cup of broth in his room—"

"No, no," Daphne assured her. "In fact, Mr. Potts intends to leave us. Indeed, I—I believe he may have done so already."

"To leave us!" echoed Mrs. Drinkard, dismayed at the prospect of losing a boarder—or, more specifically, the rent money that boarder brought in. "But why, pray, should he? And with not a word of warning, too! It seems most unlike him."

"He had—words—with Mr. Tisdale."

"But he has been with us for two years, and Mr. Tisdale for hardly more than a fortnight! If one or the other of them must leave, it should be Mr. Tisdale!"

"You do not understand, Mama. Mr. Potts was clearly in the wrong. He made, um, unwelcome advances to me, and released me only when Mr. Tisdale intervened. It is a good thing he decided to leave on his own, and spared you the unpleasant task of insisting that he go." Something in her mother's expression suggested to Daphne that events would not have played out in quite that way. "Mama! You would not have allowed him to stay, after taking such liberties!"

"Well, but Daphne, my love, boarders who pay their rent on time aren't to be casually dismissed. Who knows how long it may be until another one comes along to take his place?"

"*Casually?* Mama, he forced his attentions on me!"

"And it was very wrong of him, to be sure! But, well, when an attractive young woman lacks the protection of a father, or even a brother, such impositions are not uncommon. You would do better in the future to avoid situations that might put you in danger. Not that I think you were ever truly in danger," Mrs. Drinkard put in quickly, "for I'm sure Mr. Potts would never do anything to harm you."

"No, he only intended to slobber all over my face and push his horrid tongue into my mouth!"

Mrs. Drinkard grimaced. "Pray do not be vulgar. I can see the incident has upset you, but I am sure you are refining a great deal too much upon what was no more than an unfortunate misunderstanding. Now, that table isn't going to set itself, you know."

Correctly interpreting this observation as a dismissal, Daphne turned to go. Upon reaching the door, however, she paused to turn back. "And what if it were Sir Valerian making such advances, Mama?"

"I'm sure Sir Valerian would never do anything so ungentlemanly—especially now that he is standing for Parliament," Mrs. Drinkard added in a more practical vein. "How fortunate it would be if he did! For then I should let him know in no uncertain terms that he had compromised you, and insist that he do his duty as a gentleman."

"What duty is that, Mama?" asked Daphne, fairly sure that she already knew.

"Why, what else? To salvage your reputation by giving you the protection of his name."

"But you feel no such inclination where Mr. Potts is concerned?"

"A fledgling lawyer who won't take silk for a decade or

more? *If* he ever reaches the heights of his profession at all, which is by no means certain. Good heavens, no! I wonder you should have to ask such a thing! Sometimes I wonder about you, Daphne, truly I do."

Mrs. Drinkard was still shaking her head over her daughter's recalcitrance as Daphne left the kitchen with the stack of plates.

Dinner was an uncomfortable meal, as old Mrs. Jennings and Mr. Nethercote had to be informed (the latter several times, and in a loud voice) that Mr. Potts would no longer be residing there. Then, too, there was Mrs. Drinkard's obvious displeasure with Theo. Fortunately, neither of their elderly boarders inquired as to the nature of his infraction, being too caught up with the unexpected luxury of dining on sirloin of beef (two days old already, and thus had from the butcher at a very good price) to take notice of anything else. Whatever the cause of their inattention, Daphne could not but be grateful for it.

Any hope that Mr. Tisdale was unaware of his fall from grace, however, was dashed after the meal had ended. The company rose from the table with much scraping of chairs, but when the other boarders left the room to repair to the common drawing room or their individual bedchambers, Theo hung back.

"Yes, Mr. Tisdale?" Uncomfortably aware of her heart hammering against her ribs, Daphne averted her gaze and focused all her attention on the stacking of now-dirty plates. "Was there something you wanted?"

Following her example, Theo busied himself with

collecting the empty wineglasses. "Only to ask, if I dare, what I have done to put myself in your mother's black books."

She sighed. "You have deprived us of a paying resident—and one, moreover, who, unlike poor Mrs. Jennings, is never late with his rent."

"Have I?" Theo asked in some consternation. "But surely you must have told her why—"

"Yes," Daphne said in a flat voice. "I told her."

"And?" he prompted.

"And she says young women who have no father or brother to protect them must learn not to be shocked by such impertinences."

Theo, stunned by such maternal negligence, could only stare at her. "The devil she did!"

"To be fair, I think she did not know exactly what else to say," Daphne acknowledged. "For she is quite right, you know. Women have little enough recourse as it is, and under the circumstances—" she broke off, shrugging.

Theo considered his own sister. Even before her marriage, he couldn't imagine any man dealing Lady Helen Radney such an insult, but not because of anything he or his father might have done in retaliation. No, if anyone had tried such a thing, Nell would have—would have—

"You need to learn to defend yourself," he pronounced.

She looked up from gathering the used silverware. "I beg your pardon?"

"You need to learn to defend yourself," he said again. "I'm glad I was able to come to your aid today, but I might not be there next time."

"Perhaps Mama is wrong, and there won't be a 'next time,' " Daphne said, with more hope than conviction.

Theo shook his head. "Meaning no disrespect, Miss Drinkard, but have you looked in a mirror lately?"

As the significance of this question dawned, Daphne became very busy with the collecting of crumpled linen serviettes.

"I meant no offense," Theo said, moving around the table to open the door so that she might pass through, "but if it is as your mother said, and you must learn to expect this sort of treatment, then it behooves you to know how to protect yourself. I can show you how. After all, I once—" He broke off abruptly. *I once popped a hit over Gentleman Jackson's guard*, he'd almost said. Although this gratifying experience had been the envy of all the bucks and Corinthians who had been present on that occasion, it was unlikely that a mill worker should ever have had occasion to feel this particular thrill.

"You once—?" Daphne prompted, when he seemed disinclined to finish.

"I once acquitted myself rather well during a dust-up at the mill," said Theo, improvising rapidly.

"I see," she said, regarding him thoughtfully. "But I don't think that was what you were going to say."

"No, but it wouldn't be fit for a lady's ears," he assured her. "Tell me, is there somewhere we could meet after we take these things down to the kitchen? I can teach you how to make very short work of any future Mr. Pottses."

Daphne considered the question. "Papa's study is seldom

used," she said at last. "But you need not go down to the kitchen with me. If you will set those glasses down, I shall come back up and fetch them in a trice."

"Never!" he declared. "What if some lecherous fellow should be lurking on the stairs waiting to accost you, and you not yet trained in the art of self-defense? I should never forgive myself."

She giggled a little at that, and allowed herself, against her better judgment, to be persuaded. It really would not do to continue to hope for what could never be, to say nothing of the unfairness to Mr. Tisdale in encouraging him to think she was free to return any very obliging sentiments he might feel for her. And yet, if Mama were right, and she must expect gentlemen to treat her as a lightskirt, surely it would only be wise to learn the most effective way of acquainting them with their error. She preceded Theo through the green baize door and down the stairs to the kitchen. Cook, busy filling the large basin with water for washing the dishes, looked up at their entrance, but although she regarded Theo curiously, she offered no comment.

With the two of them working together, the table was cleared very quickly, and it seemed no time at all before they entered the small room that had been her father's study, and Theo closed the door behind them. Given the events of early evening, she should have felt extremely uncomfortable being alone with a man. But she did not—at least, not any longer— and her very lack of any such qualms was enough to make her uncomfortable.

"Now," Theo pronounced, "for your first lesson—" For

one mad moment, Daphne thought he was about to kiss her himself. She felt extremely foolish, and strangely disappointed, when he only said, "You should never have threatened to box his ears. All you did was put up his guard."

"He'd guarded himself pretty well already," she recounted bitterly. "I couldn't have boxed his ears in any case, for he'd pinned my arms to my sides."

"My dear girl, why do you think he'd pinned them there?"

"Do you mean," she asked in growing indignation, "that he immobilized me *on purpose?*"

"From his perspective, he'd have been a fool not to," Theo pointed out. "After all, you'd given him no reason to expect that you would welcome his attentions. Surely he must have known to expect some measure of resistance."

"Well! I confess, I had been feeling a bit guilty about Mr. Potts, and the way his departure must grieve Mama, but I shan't feel guilty any longer! But tell me, what should I have done? I couldn't box his ears, but I couldn't slap his face, either. What can one do, without the use of one's hands— stamp his foot, perhaps?"

"Only if you wanted to give him a good laugh," Theo said with brutal candor. "If he was wearing boots, it's unlikely he would have felt it much."

"What should I have done, then?" Daphne asked eagerly.

Theo hesitated, conscious for the first time of the degree of delicacy required in explaining to a gently reared young lady the intricacies of kneeing a man in the groin. "There's a particular area of, er, a man's anatomy that is particularly susceptible to—let us say, attack."

"And I should hit him there?" Daphne balled one fist in anticipation. "But where is it?"

"Not with your hands," Theo objected, suppressing a shudder. "They're pinned to your sides, remember?"

"Then *what?*" she demanded impatiently.

"You need to lift your knee very suddenly—your skirts are not so straight as to hamper such a movement, are they?— and catch him in the, er, between his legs."

Daphne, who had been anticipating some far more dramatic display of pugilistic skill, found these instructions rather disappointing. "That's it? That's all?"

"It will be enough, I assure you."

She regarded him doubtfully. "And that will make him release me?"

"It will make him drop to his knees and wish he'd never been born," was Theo's emphatic reply. "But you mustn't dither, and for God's sake, *don't* warn him of what you're about to do! Just jerk your knee up, and make sure the movement is quick and hard—er, forceful," amended Theo, wondering why he had ever thought this was a good idea. "Now, we'd better get out of here before your mother begins to wonder at your absence and comes looking for you."

"But—but hadn't I better practice first?"

"Good God, no!" exclaimed Theo, taking a hasty step backwards, just in case she should feel compelled to put this new skill to the test. In a gentler voice, he added, "I daresay your mother is wrong, and you'll never have to actually use it. Few men have reason to come here at all, and even if they did—well, anyone can look at you and tell you're a lady, in spite of your reduced circumstances."

She gave him a little smile. "Thank you, Mr. Tisdale."

"You're welcome, Miss Drinkard."

She made no further attempt to detain him, and waited fully ten minutes before following him from the study, lest her mother see and deduce that they had been closeted together. She was obliged to pour tea in the drawing room that night, and no one seeing her perform this task for the other residents would have believed her to have noticed, much less felt any disappointment, that Theo had chosen to seek his bed before the tea tray was sent up. And yet she lay awake in her bed long into the night, hearing again in her mind his voice asking, *Have you looked in a mirror lately?* and thinking to herself, *Mr. Tisdale thinks I'm pretty.*

12

One good turn deserves another.
GAIUS PATRONIUS, *Satyricon*

As he set out for the mill the following morning, Theo was conscious of a sense of reluctance that had little to do with the long hours of drudgery that awaited him there. No, this new disinclination concerned Miss Drinkard. He was aware, in a way he had not been before, of the precariousness of her position. He supposed there must be young women all over England who were just so uncomfortably placed; he had never really thought about it before. Because his sister had always seemed well able to take care of herself, he had assumed (if he had ever considered the matter at all) that any female of mettle would be equally competent. It had never occurred to him that Lady Helen's independence had owed as much, and quite possibly more, to her father's position as it did to her own sharp tongue.

Not, he told himself firmly, that Miss Drinkard stood in any real danger now that Mr. Potts was gone, for he could not believe old Mr. Nethercote or the middle-aged curate, Mr.

Nutley, posed any threat. Granted, Sir Valerian Wadsworth hung about the house more than Theo could like, but as he was standing for Parliament, he was unlikely to cross the line of what was proper; aside from the fact that he would want to remain in Mrs. Drinkard's good graces in order to use her house for his meetings, he would not want to risk his candidacy with charges of shameful conduct.

About Mr. Potts, though . . .

Mr. Potts could not go far, as he must needs remain within easy reach of his employer's chambers. Theo's brow creased at the thought of the aspiring lawyer. What a cabbage-head! Theo had always assumed it must take brains to read for the law, but apparently he was mistaken in this assumption; anyone but a regular clunch must have known that, if a female did not already return one's sentiments, forcing unwelcome attentions upon her was unlikely to inspire her to do so. Not that Theo believed Mr. Potts's actions had been inspired by the tender passion. No, he suspected the fellow's pursuit of Miss Drinkard had more to do with ownership than affection: Mr. Potts just wanted to prove to everyone else at the boardinghouse, and perhaps everyone in the surrounding countryside, that she was *his*.

Theo's frown deepened at this last, for it sounded uncomfortably familiar. His own sentiments toward his erstwhile mistress, La Fantasia, had not, after all, been so very different. His securing of Fanny's favors had made him the envy of every buck and blade in Town; he'd been aware of this highly gratifying fact every time he had squired her to the theatre, or Vauxhall, or any of the Cyprian's balls where gentlemen of fashion could show off their current bits of muslin (or sniff about for new ones) unencumbered by the delicate sensibilities of wives or sisters. And yet he had never for one moment considered offering her marriage; indeed, he would have scoffed at the notion that he ought to have done so. Even their very public split had inspired no sense of heartbreak, or even of any real pain beyond that of deeply wounded pride.

He was still frowning when he entered the mill and took his place at the power loom.

"Something troubling you?" asked Tom, looking up from feeding thread into the loom with calloused yet nimble fingers.

Theo shook his head, banishing the frown in the process. "Not troubled, exactly. I was just—thinking."

"Won't do to be daydreaming," Tom cautioned him.

"What's going on here?" demanded Wilkins, causing both men to jump as he came up behind them. It was a mystery to Theo how such a big man could move so silently. A natural gift for shiftiness, he supposed. Or, more practically, the noise from the looms drowned out the sounds of approaching footsteps.

"Tom here was giving me a bit of advice," Theo said smoothly. "I asked him for help. Still learning my way, you know."

Wilkins glared at him, but could hardly reprimand him for wanting to do his job more efficiently, nor Tom for assisting him in this ambition. "Ought to've learnt it by this time," he muttered, then, apparently realizing the weakness of this argument, added a bit more forcefully, "Anyway, that's enough talking, both of you. You're not being paid to chatter like magpies."

As Wilkins stalked away, Theo gave Tom a conspiratorial grin. Tom, however, met this with a slight frown and a barely discernable shake of the head as he glanced back to observe the foreman's departure. "You really mustn't do anything to provoke him, Tisdale."

"He's not paying us any heed, not any longer," Theo pointed out. "No doubt he's off in search of some other poor blighter to torment."

"So you would think," Tom acknowledged without much conviction. "But he has ways of knowing."

"Spies?" Theo glanced about the cavernous space, but the only men within his range of vision were all apparently hard at work.

"I've said too much already," Tom demurred hastily. "If we don't want to bring down his wrath on our heads, we'd best get back to work."

Theo would have asked what, if anything, Tom knew about the meetings held at the boardinghouse, but he had the distinct impression that his co-worker's lips were sealed on any subject that might make him a target of Wilkins's displeasure.

Once again, Theo wondered at his brother-in-law's allowing such a state of affairs to continue. When he had dispatched his letter to London, Theo had fully expected Sir Ethan to descend upon the mill in righteous indignation, breathing fire and losing no time in turning the odious Wilkins out on his ear. But there had been no sign of him at all, nor had Theo received any letter in response. Granted, his brother-in-law might not wish to give anyone cause to wonder why a common laborer should be receiving letters from the owner of the mill in which he toiled, but surely there were other, less direct ways of informing Theo that his correspondence had been received; it was the least he could do, Theo thought in some annoyance, given the clandestine methods he had been forced to employ in sending the damned thing.

Was it possible that the letter had never reached him? Had it been lost somewhere en route to London? Or, more ominously, had Wilkins or one of his cronies somehow intercepted it, guessed at its contents, and made certain that it never reached its destination?

"You'd best have a care, my lad," Theo chided himself under his breath, "you're beginning to sound as fearful as Tom there."

"Eh?" called Tom, cupping one hand about his ear in an approximation of an ear trumpet. "What's that?"

Theo shook his head. "Never mind."

He was still pondering the question when work was temporarily suspended for noon refreshment. He could do no more than nod at Ben, as there were no vacant seats at the long table where the older man sat. Instead, Theo took a place next to a very young man—no more than a boy, really—at the opposite end of the room.

"Do you mind if I join you?" he asked the youth, a towheaded lad of, Theo thought, about fourteen.

"Suit yourself."

The words were, perhaps, unpromising, but as he lost no time in rearranging the bread, cheese, and pickles before him in such a manner as to make more room on the table, Theo felt no compunction in stepping over the bench and plopping down upon it. He was generally considered by the *ton* to possess a delightfully disarming smile, and he now bestowed this upon the boy.

"Whew! It feels good to get off my feet."

"You'll get used to it," his tablemate assured him.

"Theo Tisdale," he said, offering his hand. "How long have you worked here, then?"

"Davy Williams," said the boy, returning his handshake. "I been here almost two years, ever since I was twelve."

"Oh?" asked Theo in some surprise. "I thought E—that is, I'd heard Sir Ethan wouldn't put children to work in his mill."

"No more he won't, usually," Davy said with some pride, as if he had accomplished no small feat in achieving employment despite this prohibition. "But when Da passed, Ma had no way to put bread on the table without I should go to work, since I'm the eldest. So Sir Ethan gimme a job, but first he made me prove to him that I could read good enough to be leaving school. Read the whole first chapter of John right out of the Bible, I did."

Theo made suitably admiring noises, but privately thought that, however skillful his reading might be, Davy's grammar could have used additional work. Theo confessed that he, too, had recently lost his father, and having established this bond, they conversed for some time on the topic of family (a seemingly innocuous subject on which Theo was hard-pressed to form answers that contained, as much as possible, some modicum of truth) until he finally posed the question that most interested him.

"What about these meetings at Mrs. Drinkard's board-inghouse?" He jerked a thumb in the general direction of his residence. "Have you been to any of them?"

Davy was instantly on his guard. "I been to the first," he admitted warily.

"Do you plan to go tonight?" Seeing that his new friend was reluctant to commit himself, Theo added, "I've been wondering whether I should attend, since I live at the boardinghouse and work at the mill. I've a foot in both camps, so to speak."

It was a tactical error, for Davy seized upon this new subject at once. "Oh, you live there? What d'you think of that Miss Daphne? She's a looker, ain't she?"

"She is, indeed. In fact, I wonder if I should attend tonight's meeting myself, just to make sure she is treated with the degree of respect that her birth, if not her current circumstances, ought to entitle her."

There was an edge to Theo's voice, but his purpose was accomplished. Davy had nothing more to say on the subject of Miss Drinkard, for his mind was once more fully fixed on the meeting itself. "I—I don't think I would, if I were you."

"Oh? Why not?"

Davy glanced about wildly as if seeking for help, but none of the men seated around them seemed to be paying the slightest heed to their conversation. "Well, it's just that—that it's not the sort of thing you'd likely enjoy."

"A dead bore, is it?" Theo asked knowingly.

"Aye, that's the thing," Davy said, seizing upon this excuse. "Just a bunch of men carping about how ill-used they are. You wouldn't like it at all."

Theo would have encouraged him to enlarge upon this theme, but at that moment the bell clanged, calling them back to work. Biting back an oath, Theo rose to his feet. He would have liked to discover more about the nature of the men's grievances, to say nothing of just how they intended to set about demanding redress. One thing, however, was becoming increasingly clear: One way or another, it behooved him to discover exactly what was going on in Mrs. Drinkard's dining room.

* * *

In the end, this ambition was made a great deal easier by the innocent machinations of Miss Drinkard, who, upon his return to the boardinghouse, waylaid him as he climbed the stairs to his bedchamber.

"Oh, Mr. Tisdale!"

He paused with one hand on the banister and smiled down at her. "Good evening, Miss Drinkard. I understand Sir Valerian is to hold another of his meetings here after dinner. I hope you are not too inconvenienced by them."

"No—that is, I fear we cannot allow our boarders to linger over their dinners, but everyone has been very obliging, so if *you* do not object—you and the others, that is—then I am sure *I* must have no cause for complaint."

No cause for complaint. She wore a coarse cotton apron

over her workaday gown of faded muslin, and her dark curls were confined, not entirely successfully, beneath a frilled mobcap better suited to a much older woman—or a servant, Theo thought, suddenly indignant on her behalf, that the daughter of the house should be forced to wait upon a set of persons less well-born than she was herself. And yet she, bless her, claimed to have no cause for complaint. He thought she was very probably the bravest person he had ever known. He supposed he must hope, for her sake, that her mother's fondest wish would be realized and some eligible suitor would appear and whisk her off to his castle in Spain. But he was not as noble as she; he hoped this paragon would not appear too soon, for her presence was the only thing that made his present situation bearable. Mrs. Drinkard had been waiting for three years; surely she could wait just a little bit longer, until his father's will had been probated and he was free to return to London.

The thought of Mrs. Drinkard served to remind Theo of the need to make haste. "*You* may not, but your mother will have a great deal of cause for complaint if I keep you all waiting on your dinners. But I believe you had something to say to me?"

"Yes." She darted a quick glance around the hall, then, finding no one within earshot, hurried up the stairs to join him. "It's about the meeting. When Sir Valerian stopped by this afternoon to check on the arrangements, I suggested he might like to have someone to take notes of whatever business they discuss. Since it's likely that at least some of the men at the mill can't read or write, I recommended you for the task. I could do no less, after—after what you did yesterday for me. With Mr. Potts, I mean." Color bloomed in her cheeks at the memory, but her voice was firmer as she added, with some urgency, "Only think, Mr. Tisdale—if Sir Valerian should be pleased with you, it could lead to your being offered a permanent position as his secretary!"

On that earlier occasion when she had first proposed that he should seek employment with his brother-in-law's political opponent, he had found the suggestion ludicrous to the point of hilarity. Now, however, as he looked down into Daphne's bright, dark eyes, he hadn't a thought to spare for Ethan, much less Sir Valerian. Nor, for that matter, did he find anything particularly amusing about Daphne's efforts on his behalf. Instead, he found it touching that she should be concerned with helping him find some way out of his temporary difficulties, while she herself was permanently trapped in a hopeless situation, forced by circumstances to labor in a boardinghouse while her youth passed her by and her beauty faded.

"Thank you, Miss Drinkard. It was very kind of you." Obeying a sudden impulse, he added, "It's impossible for me to repay you as I ought—or as you deserve, for that matter— but I should like to try. I have a length of unbleached cotton from the mill—the blisters on my fingers had burst, and it was stained with my blood, so it couldn't be sold—and I should like you to have it. The stains might come out, or you might be able to dye it and cover them up. If not, perhaps you could think of something to use it for—stockings, perhaps, or something else that no one would see." He flushed at the sudden vision this evoked of Miss Drinkard clad in nothing but her shift—and that stained with blood from his blistered fingers, almost as if his hands had been on her. Really, Theo thought, he was no better than Mr. Potts!

Daphne, clearly unaware of just how undeserving of her kindness he was, gave a little gurgle of laughter. "Stockings are knitted, Mr. Tisdale, not woven."

"What? Oh, yes—I suppose they would have to be, wouldn't they? Still, maybe you can think of—something— to do with it. Of course, if you don't want it, you don't have to—I could always—"

"Surely you don't intend to withdraw the offer, after having made it! No, Mr. Tisdale, I should like very much to have the fabric. As for what I shall do with it, why, making that decision will be half the fun!"

It was clear enough that few pleasures came her way, and Theo was glad to have given her one, no matter how small. Alas, Mrs. Drinkard's determination to hurry her boarders through dinner made it impossible for him to make good on his promise immediately, and he supposed that by the time Sir Valerian's meeting broke up, the night would be too far advanced to do so. After making these observations aloud, he promised to deliver the fabric to her the next day upon his return from the mill.

"Now, if you will excuse me, I must wash up for dinner." In a more serious vein, he added, "Thank you again for advocating for me with Sir Valerian." After a moment's awkward pause, he took her hand and pressed it to his lips.

She made no attempt to detain him, but when, some

minutes later, Mrs. Drinkard was obliged to leave the kitchen and go in search of her absentee daughter, she found the truant standing halfway up the stairs, nursing the back of one hand to her cheek.

13

The people are a many-headed beast.
HORACE, *Epistles*

Just as before, Mrs. Drinkard rushed her boarders through their evening meal in order to prepare the dining room for Sir Valerian and his gathering of mill workers. Miss Drinkard, Theo noticed, had done something different with her hair. He was not familiar enough with ladies' hairdressing to put a name to the difference, but he was apparently not the only one to take notice.

"Why, Daphne, how fetching you look tonight!" tittered Mrs. Drinkard with a coy smile. "Dare we speculate as to the reason for your new coiffure?"

Daphne, blushing crimson, stammered something about having copied it from an old issue of the *Ladies' Monthly Museum* which the squire's wife had been so obliging as to lend her.

"Sir Valerian, you know, has been most particular in his attentions," Mrs. Drinkard confided to the entire table in a whisper that might have been heard even by old Mr.

Nethercote.

Theo might have cautioned his hostess that no aspirant to a seat in the Commons would entertain thoughts of marriage to a lady with neither fortune nor connections to aid him in achieving his ambitions. But as he had no desire to embarrass Daphne even further (much less knowing of no way to express these sentiments that would not sound insulting in the extreme), he could only hope that Miss Drinkard did not share her mother's hopes regarding Sir Valerian.

When Mrs. Drinkard rose to signal the end of the meal, Theo did not repair to his bedchamber, as was his usual practice, but lingered in the drawing room with the others to await the parliamentary candidate's arrival. On this occasion, Daphne had been excused from clearing the table; Theo could only suppose her mother dared not run the risk of having Sir Valerian catching sight of her engaged in so menial an occupation.

They had not long to wait before the door knocker sounded. As Mrs. Drinkard employed no footman, much less a butler, Daphne excused herself to answer it, and returned a moment later with Sir Valerian in tow. The aspiring Member of Parliament was all affability, bowing to Mr. Nethercote as if he were visiting royalty and raising Mrs. Jennings's hand to his lips with what Theo considered an oily grace, assuring the elderly lady that she grew lovelier every time he saw her and determinedly ignoring the fact that the rings on her fingers were badly in need of cleaning. At length he turned his too-bright smile onto Theo.

"I don't believe I've had the pleasure, Mr.—?" he

inquired, offering his hand.

"Tisdale. Theodore Tisdale." Some demon of mischief led him to add, "And you are—?"

He had the satisfaction of seeing the man's smile grow rather brittle. "Sir Valerian Wadsworth, sir, your very obedient servant."

Daphne gave Theo a rather reproachful smile, but addressed herself to the parliamentary candidate. "Sir Valerian, Mr. Tisdale is the one I told you about."

"Ah, I see! I believe you are to serve as my secretary tonight, Mr. Tisdale."

"That is my understanding," said Theo, inclining his head.

Daphne led them to the dining room, which had undergone a hasty transformation since dinner. The dirty dishes had all been removed and the soiled tablecloth stripped from the table, replaced with a clean one that showed only the slightest evidence of having been darned. Although Mrs. Drinkard could not bring herself to bestow the contents of her late husband's cellars on a group of mill workers, neither could her instinct for hospitality tolerate the prospect of not offering Sir Valerian's guests any refreshment at all. A compromise had clearly been reached in the pitchers of barley water that stood at each end of the table and the second-best crystal glasses positioned at intervals corresponding to the placement of the chairs.

"If there is anything else you need, Sir Valerian, you know you have only to ask," Daphne assured him. "Now, if you will excuse me, I shall leave you alone to make whatever further preparations are needed."

Having delivered herself of this speech, she hesitated, clearly hoping for an invitation to stay. But as she received no encouragement beyond a rather bland smile from Theo and a nod of dismissal from Sir Valerian, she was left with nothing to do but dip a curtsey and betake herself from the room. After the door had closed behind her, Sir Valerian withdrew a small notebook and pencil from the inside pocket of his coat.

"You may take notes in this, Mr.—Tisdale, was it?" His brow puckered. "I say, you look deuced familiar. Have we met before, by any chance?"

Theo, assuring him that they had never met, recalled his oft-remarked-upon resemblance to his sister, and thought it much more likely that Sir Valerian had at some point glimpsed Lady Helen Brundy; perhaps she had even been pointed out to him as the wife of his opponent.

"There is one more thing," Sir Valerian said, lowering his voice. "Anything that is said in this meeting, either by myself or any of the men, is to be kept in strictest confidence. Is that understood?"

Theo assured him that he understood this caveat very well.

"Excellent! Miss Drinkard assured me that I might rely on you."

"I should not like Miss Drinkard to be disappointed," Theo said, "in either of us."

"No, of course not." Sir Valerian dismissed Daphne with an impatient shake of his head. "Let's see, what else? Would you care for some barley water? Never touch the stuff myself, but I've no objection if others do. Ah! If I'm not mistaken here comes the first arrival now."

He was not mistaken. The heavy tread of a large man sounded in the hall beyond, and a moment later Abel Wilkins entered the room. He appeared momentarily taken aback by Theo's presence, but made a quick recovery.

"Well, if it isn't Thee-o-dore," he said, his lip curling in a sneer.

"I believe you know Mr. Tisdale," Sir Valerian put in smoothly. "He has agreed to take notes for us this evening."

Wilkins looked less than pleased with this revelation, but raised no objection. Theo suspected he was afraid of running counter to Sir Valerian's wishes, and thought it rather ironic that one who didn't hesitate to bully the dozens of mill workers under his supervision should himself be cowed by a fellow of whom any one of a dozen gentlemen of his acquaintance (to say nothing of his own brother-in-law) would have made very short work.

A number of mill workers arrived in Wilkins's wake, including the boy Davy Williams, who shot Theo a look that was both sheepish and reproachful. Although Theo could not have put a name with even half of the dozen or so men crowded about Mrs. Drinkard's table, he recognized most of their faces, and they obviously recognized him—and were none too pleased to see him there, if the suspicious looks with which they regarded him were anything to judge by.

Sir Valerian, perhaps aware of the general air of disapprobation, announced to the group at large, "Mr. Tisdale is acting as my secretary tonight. Naturally, I have cautioned him as to the need for the utmost discretion. He will not repeat anything he hears within these four walls."

The devil I won't, thought Theo, bestowing upon the group a bland smile.

His intention had been to write at once to Sir Ethan in London, informing his brother-in-law of any havey-cavey dealings by his opponent and trusting that this second letter would not go amiss, as had, apparently, the first. But it soon transpired that there was little, if anything, to report. Indeed, the order of the day appeared to be the planning of an autumn festival for the mill workers and their families, since Lady Helen Brundy, who usually hosted just such an event, was currently in mourning for her father.

"I've spoken to the squire, and he is willing to let us use his barn for the occasion," Sir Valerian informed the group.

"Aye, that's all right," put in one of the men, nodding in approval. "It's near enough to the mill to be reached quick enough, even in the dark, but not so close as to arouse any suspicions."

Several of the men shifted uneasily in their chairs, and Davy's gaze dropped to stare fixedly at the tablecloth. Sir Valerian said, with a hint of steel in his voice that had not been there before, "I don't know why you should think there would be any need for 'suspicions,' Ainsworth. What could anyone find objectionable in a simple night of music and dancing? Unless, of course, you intend to partake a bit too freely of the liquid refreshment, and don't want your wife to know."

It seemed to Theo that all the men laughed a bit too heartily at this witticism, but he was forced to agree with Sir

Valerian. True, the man was taking advantage of his opponent's bereaved status in order to ingratiate himself with the locals, but that wasn't objectionable in and of itself; all was fair in love and politics, after all, and these men would not be able to vote in any case, so Theo failed to see what Sir Valerian hoped to gain by this show of generosity. In any case, the highest sticklers—who *could* vote—would certainly hold it against Ethan if he were to fail to show the proper respect for his father-in-law's passing, so Theo was inclined to think his sister was right in not hosting the event.

"Of course, I will need a lady to act as hostess," Sir Valerian continued, glancing at Theo to make sure he was committing all these details to paper. "I hope to persuade Mrs. Drinkard to oblige me in this, as she has been so gracious in allowing me to hire her dining room."

Theo frowned a little over his writing. Surely it was unnecessary to belittle the lady by betraying to these men that she was being compensated for her hospitality. Or did he mean to hint that Mrs. Drinkard's straitened circumstances gave him some hold over her? If so, Theo could assure him that no such coercion was necessary; Mrs. Drinkard would no doubt be over the moon to be returned, even if only for one night, to what should have been her proper sphere.

Nor would she be the only one. As the details were discussed of what musicians were available locally to play for the dancing, as well as what food and drink should be procured from whom, Theo was a bit taken aback by the air of suppressed excitement underlying the preparations. In his experience, most men were content to leave the finer points of entertaining to their wives, while as for attending such events, the general lack of enthusiasm with which the male of the species regarded them was the bane of hostesses throughout London. He supposed, without much conviction, that such pleasures rarely came these men's way. Yes, that must account for it. For there was no denying the intensity on the faces of the men seated around the table, as if they were plotting a military campaign instead of a night of revelry.

The only exception appeared to be Davy Williams, who spoke up at one point to say, "I don't know—I think maybe we ought'n't to—" Seeing that every man in the room (every man except Theo, anyway) was regarding him with thinly veiled hostility, he continued in a quavering voice, "That is, what I mean to say is, Sir Ethan's been that good to me after my old man died. I—I wouldn't want to do anything he wouldn't like."

Sir Valerian bent a rather brittle smile upon him. "That's quite all right—Davy, is it? I'm sure no one is asking you to do anything you don't want to do. You're welcome to leave us right now, if you so choose."

There followed an uncomfortable silence. Davy slumped down in his chair and mumbled, "I'll stay, sir."

"Very wise of you," commended Sir Valerian. He glanced at Theo and nodded slightly, giving his secretary to understand that he was to make a notation of the boy's unwillingness. With considerable reluctance, Theo wrote, *Davy Williams voiced his objection to*—to what? Granted, when Theo had been Davy's age, he wouldn't have submitted meekly to an evening of doing the pretty when he might have been more agreeably occupied in riding hell-for-leather over the countryside, or bagging a rabbit or a partridge or two. But there seemed to be more to Davy's reluctance than a youth's indifference to a night of dancing. —*to the plan*, Theo wrote.

Alas, he was no more enlightened when the meeting broke up several hours later. He didn't know if the men were being particularly careful of how much they said within his hearing, or if they were merely a bit embarrassed at their own unmanly enthusiasm for an event that should have held more appeal for their wives and daughters than for themselves. This might account for their displeasure at his presence, and Sir Valerian's need to reassure them as to Theo's discretion. And yet, Theo could not quite forget Mr.—Ainsworth's, was it?— comment about "suspicions," and how quickly this suggestion was quashed by Sir Valerian. No, more than ever he was convinced that there was some more sinister purpose to the meetings. He had no very firm idea of what that purpose might be, but of one thing he was certain.

Daphne and her mother must be kept out of it.

* * *

Theo had no opportunity to speak to Daphne that night, as she had already sought her bed by the time the meeting was adjourned, but he resolved to do so as soon as he returned from the mill the following day. With any luck, he would reach her before Sir Valerian had an opportunity to speak to her mother about acting as his hostess. If at all possible, Mrs. Drinkard must be persuaded not to become any more deeply embroiled in the enterprise (whatever it was) than she was already. He did not envy Daphne the task; from what he knew of her mother, that lady would not willingly give up her chance either to play the Lady Bountiful or to drag her daughter along willy-nilly in an attempt to fix Sir Valerian's interest.

When he reached the mill, he discovered that somehow the word had got out that he had joined the conspirators, if conspirators they were. Responses to his new status were mixed. Wilkins regarded him with, if hardly affection, then surely less hostility than he had previously done, and several of the other men who had been present now greeted him with terse nods that acknowledged him as one of their number while at the same time discouraging him from making any reference to the meeting or what had been discussed there. Tom, on the other hand, had withdrawn from him, saying no more than was strictly necessary for the sake of civility. Davy Williams had not come to work at all; Theo found his absence ominous without precisely knowing why.

When the noon break came, Theo sought out a place beside Old Ben, who greeted him with a rather curt nod.

"Not you, too!" Theo exclaimed in some dismay. "Ever since I arrived at the mill this morning, half the men here have been treating me like I'm some kind of leper."

"And the other half?" Regarding him speculatively, Ben thawed only somewhat. "How have they been treating you?"

Theo gave a bitter laugh. "They're not openly hostile, like Tom and the rest, but it's plain as a pikestaff they don't trust me. You'd think I'd turned spy."

"Haven't you?"

Theo had the grace to blush. "In fact, I only attended the

173

meeting to oblige a lady. I'd helped her out of a rather tight spot, and she'd thought to repay me by helping me get a position as Sir Valerian Wadsworth's secretary, beginning with my taking notes during the meeting last night." It was the truth, so far as it went. What he didn't say was that, had Miss Drinkard not given him the entrée, he'd had every intention of eavesdropping through the chimney flue. Spying, in fact.

"So"—Ben leaned forward, dropping his voice to a near-whisper—"what do they do at those meetings, anyway?"

"Just a bunch of men airing their grievances," Theo said with a shrug, falling back on Davy's description. "Oh, and it appears Sir Valerian is going to host a party for the mill workers and their families, since Nell—that is, since Lady Helen Brundy can't do it, being in mourning as she is. The men all seemed over the moon about that, so perhaps they'll be less prone to complain in the future."

"Is that all, then?" asked Ben, the furrows in his brow clearing. "I'd been afraid—but never mind that. Young Davy seemed a mite worried about it, is all."

"Where is Davy today? Do you know?"

Ben shook his head. "No, and it's not like him to miss a day. 'In sickness or in health,' he is, like a marriage vow."

"Do you know where he lives? Perhaps I'll stop by after work and look in on him."

Ben did indeed know where Davy lived—Theo suspected there wasn't much about the village that Ben did *not* know—and, true to his word, after he left the mill that evening, Theo did not return immediately to the boarding-house, but followed Ben's directions to the cottage where

Davy lived with his mother and younger siblings.

A worn-looking woman of middle age opened the door to him and, being informed of his errand, stepped aside to allow him to enter. He did so, although the door was so low that he had to duck his head. As his eyes adjusted to the dim light within, he found himself in a room that seemed to serve as drawing room, dining room, and kitchen, all in one. A black cauldron hung from a crane in the fireplace, and something redolent of onions and garlic bubbled within. Two adolescent girls set pewter plates around the table, their lanky forms swathed in aprons that had obviously been made for their mother. At Theo's entrance, they looked up from their task with much giggling and blushing. Three smaller children stacked wooden blocks precariously on a rag rug covering the unvarnished boards of the floor.

"It's right kind of you to ask after my Davy," the woman said, making a vague gesture toward the back of the house where, presumably, Davy might be found.

"Is he ill, then?" Theo asked. "I was told that it's unusual for him to miss work."

"Ill?" she echoed in some consternation. "I see you don't know, then. No, he's not ill. He was set upon on his way home from the Drinkard place last night."

"S—Set upon?" Theo echoed stupidly.

"Aye, three men—or he says maybe it was four, he couldn't see very well on account of it being dark, and him being too busy trying to ward off blows to stop and count. They was lyin' in wait just this side of the bridge. But he can tell you himself, if he feels up to it."

Theo tried to recall the ending of the meeting. It had been quite late by the time it broke up, and he'd been impatient to go upstairs to bed, knowing he would have to get up at dawn this morning. He'd been more than a little annoyed, too, at having wasted the evening listening to a group of men planning the details of a party in which he had not the slightest interest. But he vaguely recalled Wilkins detaining Davy for a moment to ask him some work-related question about a problem that had arisen that day. Had it been a deliberate attempt to delay the boy, allowing the others time to stake out a position from which to attack him? And why should they have done so? The answer to this question, at least, was not far to seek: Theo remembered Davy's timid suggestion that they ought not to—to *what?* More than ever, Theo was convinced that something more than a party was at issue.

"I'd take you to him, excepting that I've got to get supper on the table," Davy's mother continued, glancing back at her giggling daughters.

"You need not trouble yourself," Theo assured her hastily, throwing the girls into confusion by winking at them. "I'm sure I can find my own way."

This, at least, proved to be no mystery, for the cottage was not nearly large enough to become lost in. He found Davy in one of the two bedrooms in the back of the house, and suffered a check. Davy lay flat on his back in the narrow bed with the quilt drawn up to his chin, but this was insufficient to conceal the extent of the damage. The boy's face was covered with bruises, and although he appeared to be asleep, one of his eyes was so swollen that Theo doubted he could open it in any case. Blood had dried along a cut in one cheek, and matted together the blond hair over his forehead. As Theo stood wondering whether to go or stay, Davy spoke.

"Warned you—not to go," he said, his voice scarcely more than a whisper.

"Yes, you did," Theo acknowledged ruefully, "and yet, you went yourself."

"Once you're in . . . can't get out. You'll see."

"Who did it? Do you know?"

"Couldn't see . . . in the dark. One of them . . . might have been Ainsworth. Sounded a bit like him . . . never be able to prove it, though."

"Davy . . ." Theo hesitated, uncertain how to voice the question. "What's it all about? It must be more than just a dance."

"Aye, though that bit is necessary. It's—"

He got no further, for at that moment his mother came into the room. "Dinner's ready. Do you think you could come to the table, or shall I have Molly bring it to you in a cup?"

Davy rather cautiously expressed his ability to come to the table, and Theo, seeing there were no further confidences to be got from him, judged it time to take his leave. He assured both Davy and his mother that there was no talk of replacing him at the mill, then followed Mrs. Williams from the room.

"Will he be all right?" he asked, nodding his head in the direction of the bedroom they had just vacated. "What does the doctor say?"

"We haven't had the doctor in," confessed Mrs. Williams with a sigh. "There's no money for it, especially now that my boy is out of work."

"Send for the doctor, and send the bill to me," said Theo without hesitation. Ethan had already paid several of his debts; he could jolly well stand the nonsense for one more.

Hope flared briefly in the woman's eyes before giving way to doubt. "Are you sure you can afford it, Mr.—Tisdale, was it?"

"I'm sure." Lest any further assurances were needed, he gave her his sweetest smile. "Unlike Davy, I've no one but myself to support," he said, with a silent apology to the army of servants, tenant farmers, and tin miners whose livings were subject to the Duke of Reddington's every whim.

After an initial show of reluctance, Mrs. Williams allowed herself to be persuaded, and Theo set out for the boardinghouse with, if not a mind set entirely at ease, at least the sense of well-being that generally accompanies the performance of a good deed. Alas, this gratifying state of affairs did not long survive his return to the boardinghouse, for upon reaching his temporary residence, he found Daphne in the dining room setting the table.

"Oh, Mr. Tisdale!" she exclaimed, brightening upon seeing him. "You're late this evening."

"Is your mother terribly vexed with me? One of the men who was at the meeting last night was, er, injured on his way home, so I stopped to call on him."

"That was kind of you," she said warmly. "But what happened to him? I hope he is not too badly injured."

Theo struggled for some way to reassure her without resorting to outright fabrication. "Nothing that won't heal, I trust." After a moment's hesitation, he added, "Miss Drinkard, I feel I should perhaps warn—"

"In any case, I am glad you are home now, for I have the most wonderful news! Sir Valerian Wadsworth is hosting a dance for the mill workers and their families, just as Lady Helen Brundy would have done had her father not died, and he has asked Mama to act as hostess!"

He didn't let any grass grow under his feet, Theo thought resentfully. Although he knew what answer he would get, he asked, "And what did your mother say?"

"She agreed, of course. In fact, she is quite in alt, for it is just the sort of thing she might have done if Papa were still alive. And—and I confess, I am excited at it myself, for Mama would never let me go before, even though the vicar always attended, and the doctor, and any number of quite *respectable* people in addition to the mill workers! Not that you are not respectable, of course," she added hastily, realizing too late that he might be justified in taking exception to this assessment of himself and his co-workers. "It is only that she *must* let me go now, for it would be very odd if she were to be hostess, and yet not allow me to attend! Truth to tell, after Papa died, I thought—I thought I would never be able to dance again."

Theo found her eagerness both touching and heart-breaking—all the more so because such an event would have been scorned by most of the London ladies of his acquaintance. He hadn't the heart to destroy her innocent pleasure by hinting that she might do better to stay away, never mind suggesting she assume the hopeless task of attempting to dissuade her mother from obliging Sir Valerian. In fact, all things considered, there was only one thing he could say.

"Miss Drinkard," he said with a little smile, "I hope you will honor me with the first waltz, in spite of my lack of respectability."

As if to prove himself worthy of this honor, he bowed deeply from the waist, and she responded by spreading the skirt of her apron and sinking into a curtsy.

"The honor will be all mine, sir," she said,

"I shall look forward to it," he said, and was surprised to discover that he meant it. "But now I suppose I'd best go and wash up for dinner."

He would have suited the action to the word, but she cried, "Oh, I almost forgot! A letter came for you in today's post."

Ethan! Thank God! With any luck, it would say he'd got Theo's letter and was returning hotfoot from London to sort out whatever was in the wind at his mill. Theo followed Daphne into the hall, where a couple of letters lay on the small table near the front door. To his surprise, she handed him not just one, but both of them.

"The other is for Mrs. Jennings," she explained. "Would you be kind enough to take it up to her? She has the second room on the left, on the opposite end of the corridor from you."

Theo agreed, and was soon knocking on the older lady's door. She opened it, and he surrendered the letter to her.

"This came for you in today's post," he explained. "Miss Drinkard asked me to bring it up to you."

"Thank you," she said, receiving it with hands clawed by arthritis. "Such a good boy . . . so like your poor mother."

Theo hastily denied having done anything remarkable, but returned to his room much shaken. *So like your poor mother . . .* Had Mrs. Jennings known his mother? Had she recognized him as his mother's son? It was all nonsense, of course. Mrs. Jennings was three parts senile. Granted, Theo had no very clear memory of his mother, who had died when he was still in the nursery, but if a certain painting hanging in his ancestral home was anything to judge by, he did indeed look very much like her . . .

He was still pondering the implications of Mrs. Jennings's cryptic utterance as he broke the seal on his own correspondence, but this had the effect of driving all other considerations from his mind. It was indeed from his brother-in-law, but it made no mention of the letter Theo had sent him. Instead, Ethan was (he said) pleased to inform Theo that his father's will had been granted probate, and his exile was at an end.

"I'm free," Theo murmured stupidly, staring at the paper in his hand. "I'm free to go."

14

Letting "I dare not" wait upon "I would."
WILLIAM SHAKESPEARE, *Macbeth*

Hard on the heels of his unexpected liberation came the realization that he could not take advantage of it. The vague notion that he lacked funds to arrange for the hire of a post-chaise (for he had no intention of once more subjecting his person to the rigors of travel on the common stage) was given the lie by Sir Ethan's assurances that Theo had only to present himself at his brother-in-law's bank, where instructions had been sent by that same day's post instructing that Theo was to be advanced any sum he required up to a maximum of twenty pounds sterling.

No, Theo was under no financial obligation to remain in Lancashire. Nor could he flatter himself that his departure would leave the mill understaffed, for although the quality of his work had undoubtedly improved over the course of his employment, he could not convince himself that his absence would have a negative effect on production.

Still, the fact remained that he could not leave. Not now.

It was very clear that Ethan was not coming, and although Theo could not say whether his continued absence was due to ignorance or willful neglect, it clearly behooved him, he thought with a trace of annoyance, to look after his brother-in-law's interests until such time as he could prevail upon Ethan to look after them himself.

If he were honest, however, there was another reason, one far more compelling than any sense of family loyalty toward his sister's husband. In truth, he could not leave without ensuring Miss Drinkard's safety. He was not sure exactly what plans were being hatched in her mother's dining room, but it seemed to him that Sir Valerian's party, added to Mrs. Drinkard's ambitions for her daughter, might prove to be a volatile, even an explosive combination. He could not go without first being certain Miss Drinkard came to no harm through her own quite innocent involvement.

In fact, he realized with dawning conviction, he would not have been easy in his mind about leaving Miss Drinkard even had her home *not* been being used for some nefarious purpose; the sight of her struggling in the embrace of Mr. Potts had been enough to see to that. Theo had been vaguely conscious of a desire to kiss Miss Drinkard ever since the night she had come up to his room to bandage his blistered hands. Any such inclinations, however, had been fairly easy to hold at bay: Miss Drinkard was not the sort of female with whom one could trifle, and even had his intentions toward her been serious, it would not do to press a suit which, so long as he continued in his present guise, she would be compelled to discourage.

And then had come Mr. Potts. While Theo did that ardent young man the justice to own that his advances had very likely been made with marriage in mind, he had been infuriated to discover that Mr. Potts apparently felt no compunctions in taking by force those liberties that Theo would not allow himself to pursue even by subtler means. His indignation had been considerably exacerbated by the realization that his own intentions toward Miss Drinkard were very serious indeed.

But what to do? He flattered himself that she would not find his attentions so objectionable as those of the odious Mr. Potts, but if he were to declare himself to her, he would put her in an intolerable position by proposing a match which her mother could never allow, much less approve. On the other hand, if he were to reveal his true identity, she would be obliged to divulge this information to her mother, and that ambitious lady's demeanor toward him would undergo such a transformation that his position at the mill, both as a worker and as a member of the disgruntled inner circle that congregated in Mrs. Drinkard's dining room, would very quickly become untenable. Then, too, any such confession must of necessity include an explanation of the circumstances that had led to his present charade, and this, given the late Mr. Drinkard's weakness for gambling, might provoke feelings of such revulsion in Miss Drinkard's breast that any affection she might feel for him would be completely overwhelmed.

No, for a number of reasons, his best course of action— indeed, his *only* course of action—was to remain where he was, and await events.

With a sigh of mingled frustration and regret, he lit the

candle on the writing table and held the letter to the flame until it caught, then tossed the burning paper onto the grate and watched as his ticket back to London blackened and turned to ash.

* * *

In the meantime, Daphne was, with some trepidation, preparing to broach a related topic with her mother as they made the final preparations for dinner.

"—And you may bring down your ball gown from the attic, my love," her mother pronounced as she energetically sliced a freshly baked loaf of bread and spread each slice with butter.

"Oh, Mama!" Daphne cried eagerly. "Do you mean it?"

"Yes, indeed! To be sure, this is only a country party, and most of the guests barely respectable. But to appear shabby-genteel would reflect poorly on Sir Valerian. We must demonstrate to him that you are worthy of moving in the highest circles."

"Mama," Daphne began cautiously, "I feel I must warn you that while Sir Valerian might attempt to flirt with me, he has never given me the slightest indication that his gallantries are serious."

"Of course not, my dear!" exclaimed Mrs. Drinkard, clearly affronted. "He is far too well-bred to do such a thing without speaking to me first. Of course, had your poor father been alive, it would be he to whom Sir Valerian would apply for permission to address you, but as things now stand—"

"Mama!" Daphne interrupted, shock (and yes, perhaps dismay) making her forget her manners, "Do you mean that

Sir Valerian *has* spoken to you?"

"No," her mother confessed with a sigh of regret. "Still, we must not despair. I'm sure Sir Valerian must be a very busy man right now. It may not be until later, after the elections, that he has time to think of such things, and to realize the value of having a wife at his side."

Privately, Daphne thought it would be much longer than that before the aspiring M. P. thought of her in that rôle. Aloud, she merely said, "Mama, I think it would be a mistake to pin all our hopes on Sir Valerian, or to look too high for a husband for me, given our present circumstances. Indeed, there have been times of late when I have thought marriage to—to a man who is good and kind, even if he is not wealthy, might be preferable to the prospect of spinsterhood."

"You have, have you?" Mrs. Drinkard's eyes narrowed in sudden suspicion. "And are you thinking of any 'good and kind' man in particular?"

"N-no," Daphne demurred with perhaps more discretion than honesty.

"Good," declared her mother, "for I must urge you to put any such thought out of your head. Even if Sir Valerian does not come up to scratch—and I have not yet given up hope in that quarter, not by a long chalk!—you must not forget what is due your name, my dear. Why, before your poor Papa's death, you might have looked as high as—but never mind that. Matters are not so dire that you must reconcile yourself to marriage with just anyone, for you will have this house after I am gone, and well, there is never a shortage of people in need of lodging."

"And what of—of companionship, Mama?"

"My dear, surely you are aware that companionship is never a problem in a house filled with boarders!"

"That's not the kind of companionship I meant." Daphne felt her face grow warm, and knew she was blushing. "I was talking about love."

"I see," her mother said darkly, giving her an appraising look. "Don't go filling your head with romantic notions, my dear. Love may be what all the songs are about, but it rarely lasts. Indeed, when I discovered how your father had been hoaxing us all those years, and how uncomfortably he had left us, it destroyed every scrap of the affection I once felt for him!" She plunged the knife into the loaf as if it had been her late husband's heart.

Daphne hardly knew what to say, for she, too, had difficulty reconciling the loving father of her childhood memories with the hardened gambler who had left his wife and daughter penniless.

"But do not despair," her mother continued on a more positive note. "If Sir Valerian has not yet thought of marriage with you, I'm sure he will have only to see you in your proper rôle to be captivated."

"My 'proper rôle, Mama?" Daphne echoed, one dimple peeping. "A gathering of mill workers and their families?"

"Do not be impertinent, miss! You know very well what I meant. I daresay Sir Valerian may host similar gatherings for his constituents, and he needs to see that you are capable of planning such things."

"I think the men are doing all the planning, Mama,"

Daphne said, recalling certain things that Theo had let fall.

"Never mind that!" Mrs. Drinkard waved away this detail with a dismissive gesture that caused Daphne to duck out of range of the knife. "You must bring your dress down from the attic, my dear, and hang it up so that any wrinkles may fall out. I wish we might bring it down to the kitchen to steam them out, but we can't have you going to the dance reeking of garlic and onions."

"No, indeed!" exclaimed Daphne, laughing. "Although it would certainly inspire Sir Valerian to make me an offer—to serve as his cook."

"Pray do not even joke about such a thing!" Setting aside her knife, Mrs. Drinkard transferred the slices of bread to a basket lined with a checkered cloth, folded the ends of the cloth over the bread to keep it warm, and handed the whole to Daphne. "Set this on the table, my dear, and then you may go up and change. As for the dance"—she sighed—"we shall have to wait and see what happens."

* * *

" 'ow'd you like to go back 'ome for a bit, love?" Sir Ethan Brundy inquired of his spouse upon his return from his club, where he had been meeting with the principal advisors in his Parliamentary campaign.

"Ethan!" Lady Helen exclaimed, rising from her place on the sofa to greet him with a kiss. "Are you burying me in the country again?"

The joke was an old and oft-repeated one, for Lady Helen had long since discovered that the pleasures of hearth and home were, in their own quiet way, equal—and sometimes superior—to the gaieties of Town.

"Not if you think it's too soon," her husband assured her, glancing down at their son, who sat on the rug drawing in a sketch pad with a blue crayon. "Can Willie travel yet, do you think?"

"The doctor says there is no reason why he should not do so, provided we wrap him up well, for he is much improved."

This much was certainly true. In fact, the purchase of the sketch pad and crayons with which he was presently employed had been a desperate attempt on her part to give him some more suitable occupation than chasing the kitchen cat (in an attempt to grab its tail) or thrusting his head up the chimney (in order, as he explained to his sorely tried mama, to see what was there). Master William Brundy, apparently feeling their eyes upon him, judged it time to present them with the fruit of his labor: a misshapen circle with eyes, nose, and a smiling mouth, from which sticklike arms and legs sprouted without such apparent superfluities as a neck or a torso. This, he informed his bemused parents, depicted his papa.

"And a fine, 'andsome fellow I am," declared Sir Ethan without a blink, considering this highly unflattering likeness with every appearance of satisfaction. "What do you think, Willie? Would you like to go back to Lancashire?"

Willie pondered this question for a long moment before asking, "Is Charley there?"

"Aye, Charley's in Lancashire, along with Nurse and your sisters."

Sketch pad and crayon were cast aside at this news of his

twin. "I wanna see Charley!" shrieked Willie as he leaped to his feet, ready to depart on the instant.

"I confess, I have missed the other children," Lady Helen said. "But what of your debate with Sir Valerian? Was it not this Saturday?"

" 'e's canceled it," her husband informed her, bending to scoop his son up in his arms.

"Canceled it? Why should he do such a thing?"

Sir Ethan shrugged. "No idea. Per'aps 'e's sure enough of his position to believe 'e doesn't need it."

Lady Helen's bosom swelled in indignation. "Well! If *that's* what he thinks—"

" 'e's welcome to think whatever 'e likes—especially if it means we can go back 'ome and rest up for a few days before the next round of dinners and speeches," put in Sir Ethan.

"I see your point," conceded Lady Helen with a sigh. "It has been rather exhausting, hasn't it? And that in spite of the fact that our schedule has been greatly reduced since Papa died! When I think how I was used to attend three events in the same night, it quite sinks my spirits! I must be growing old."

"I'd thought we might leave in the morning and stop for the night in Leicester. We could be there by Friday night— unless you'd rather go at a slower pace, decrepit as you are."

She smiled at that, but refused to take the bait. "It might be best to take a slower pace for Willie's sake."

"We can take three days, then, stopping at Olney and Stafford instead," he suggested. "That would put us there shortly after nightfall on Saturday. 'ow's that?"

"Better," she pronounced, nodding as she rose from her seat on the sofa. "It would allow us to sleep a bit later in the mornings, too, which I confess sounds divine. But if we are to set out before noon tomorrow, I had best see about packing."

* * *

Such was the state of affairs in three different quarters when, after much anticipation, the day of Sir Valerian's party arrived.

15

Love gilds the scene, and women guide the plot.
RICHARD BRINSLEY SHERIDAN, *The Rivals*

Three years of deprivation had robbed the former belle of Lancashire of whatever vanity she had once possessed, but Daphne, regarding her reflection in the cheval mirror that took up far too much space in her tiny bedchamber, could not quite suppress a little thrill of satisfaction. The gown had not sustained any injury during its long exile, and if it was not quite as fashionable as it had been when she had first received it from the hands of the dressmaker, it was unlikely that anyone at tonight's entertainment was sufficiently *au courant* with the latest modes to recognize this.

Most of the good jewelry had been sold in the weeks following her father's death, but Daphne had managed to keep the pearls he had given her for her seventeenth birthday. These now encircled her throat, and a single pearl trembled in each ear. As for her hair, she had washed it that morning in a preparation scented with violets and brushed it until it shone. It was now piled high on her head and threaded through with pearls—false ones, alas, unlike the ones she'd been given for her birthday, but the effect was charming nonetheless—with little ringlets escaping at her temples and the nape of her neck.

She tried to calm the butterflies cavorting about in her stomach by reminding herself that this was a far cry from the court presentation that was to have been hers, but this argument was silenced by the knowledge that *he* would be there, and had claimed her for the first waltz. Under such circumstances, it was impossible to remain *blasé*; in fact, no young lady making her first appearance at Almack's had suffered a greater agitation of spirits.

Her turbulent thoughts were interrupted by a light tapping on the door, and a moment later her mother peered into the room. "Daphne, do you need any assistance? How I miss the days when I used to have a lady's maid to help with— oh, my dear!" she exclaimed in quite a different voice. "Never have I seen you in such looks! Such bright eyes! Such a rosy glow! When I think of the brilliant Season you might have had, and the match you might have made, it puts me all out of patience with—but never mind that! I am sure all that is to be put right, for Sir Valerian has only to look at you to—to—" Here she was obliged to seek recourse to the lace-edged handkerchief she carried in her sleeve.

"I'm glad you are pleased, Mama," Daphne said in a curiously flat voice. How could she tell her mother that it was not the prospect of dazzling Sir Valerian that had put the sparkle in her eyes and the color in her cheeks? Worse yet, even if her mother were to be proven right, and Sir Valerian were to make her an offer, how could she possibly accept, when her heart belonged to Mr. Tisdale? And yet, how could she not, when marriage to Sir Valerian might well be, as her mother claimed, their only chance at a better life?

* * *

Theo, in the meantime, had wrestled all week with a dilemma of his own: the question of what to wear. He could hardly send to London for his evening kit; besides giving his valet palpitations, he would have to offer his present company some explanation for his possessing clothing of such quality. And yet, he could not tolerate the thought of presenting himself to Miss Drinkard dressed in his secondhand work clothes. In the end, however, he was forced to do exactly that, selecting the better—but not by much—of his two shirts and doing his best to compensate for its shortcomings by reclaiming the cravat he'd abandoned after his first day at the mill (although its appearance might have been greatly improved by a liberal application of starch) and the plain brown tailcoat.

His toilet complete, Theo descended the stairs to the drawing room where, on this occasion, everyone was to assemble before removing to the dining room in a formal procession. The reason for this departure from the usual arrangement soon became clear: Mrs. Drinkard had invited the more respectable of Sir Valerian's party guests to dine before the event, just as if she had been hosting a ball in her own home. Once these had arrived—the squire and his lady, the doctor and his wife, the vicar along with his spinster sister and his sixteen-year-old daughter—the company paired off and progressed to the dining room, led by Mrs. Drinkard on the arm of Sir Valerian. Theo, as (apparently) the lowest in rank amongst the males of the party, offered his arm to the vicar's daughter, a well-behaved girl whose plain countenance concealed a keen intelligence. Theo, finding her disconcerting gaze upon him, rapidly calculated how long it had been since he had attended divine services with his sister and her family, and how old this unnerving young lady must have been at the time.

Upon entering the dining room, however, all such thoughts were driven from his head, for here it must have become clear to the meanest intelligence that Mrs. Drinkard, having been asked to act as hostess, intended to do the thing properly. The room had undergone a stunning transformation since the previous night's evening meal. A cloth of crisp white linen overlaid with fine Irish lace now covered the table, anchored by porcelain bowls of late chrysanthemums. Tall beeswax candles in silver candelabra (which, had Theo but known it, Daphne had spent the better part of the morning deedily employed in polishing) had been positioned at intervals down its length, whence they cast a warm golden glow over the room. The table was set with what Theo suspected must be Mrs. Drinkard's wedding crystal and china; certainly they were different, and far finer, than that on which her boarders usually partook of their meals.

Nor had the seating arrangements escaped alteration. Miss Drinkard had been ousted from her place at the end of the table opposite her mother, and Sir Valerian installed there in her stead, with Miss Drinkard on his right. In like manner, old Mr. Nethercote's traditional place at Mrs. Drinkard's right was now occupied by the squire; clearly, age and infirmity hadn't a patch on one who, besides being the holder of a baronetcy, had been so obliging as to allow Sir Valerian to hold the fête in his barn.

But more striking than all of these was the meal itself. In lavish contrast to the single course usually offered the boardinghouse residents, tonight's dinner ran to four removes, each one grander than the one before it. It began with a white soup, which yielded place to a salmon pie along with asparagus in cream sauce, followed by stuffed partridges and a potato pie. There were custards and aspics and puddings, along with fresh fruits, nuts, and cheeses.

How, Theo wondered, did Mrs. Drinkard expect to pay for it all? In the next instant, he knew. Like the deceased husband whose habits she so frequently deplored, Mrs. Drinkard was a gambler, staking all her counters on one cast of the dice: tonight Miss Drinkard was to secure a proposal of marriage from Sir Valerian. The realization gave Theo a hollow feeling in the pit of his stomach, and he found himself unable to do justice to the cook's *pièce de résistance*, as the crown roast of lamb brought Miss Drinkard's rôle of sacrificial lamb all too forcibly to his mind. As he picked at his dinner, he pondered with relish the prospect of a private interview with Mrs. Drinkard, during which he would reveal his identity and request her permission to pay his addresses to her daughter. But any satisfaction he might have derived from this pleasant fantasy was considerably dampened by the realization that, so long as he remained in his present circumstances, his hands were tied. Damn Ethan! What was taking him so long? At this rate, Sir Valerian would be posting the banns before Theo was at liberty to speak to Daphne at all.

Such was Theo's state of mind when Mrs. Drinkard at last rose from the table, signaling the end of the meal. The ladies of the party followed her lead, as did the gentlemen, who in deference to the occasion forewent the custom of postprandial port. Sir Valerian had already arranged to transport the Drinkard ladies to the fête in his own carriage, and the vicar gave the curate a seat in his gig, but although the squire and his wife offered to take up Mrs. Jennings in their antiquated landau, that lady was resolute in her refusal—so much so that more than one member of the party wondered if the poor old dear was growing senile. Once the carriages had set out, however, she turned to regard Theo, her eyes bright with intelligence and purpose.

"At last!" she declared. "I thought they would never go. Come upstairs at once, for we haven't much time."

"I—I beg your pardon?" Theo asked, all at sea.

"So much like your dear mama, God rest her soul," recalled Mrs. Jennings with a reminiscent sigh. "But we haven't much time, not if we're to save Daphne from that odious young man. Did you see the way he looked at her? I thought he was going to eat her along with the sweets course."

Theo had indeed seen, and had found the sight every bit as repugnant as Mrs. Jennings had. "But—what are we going to do?"

Mrs. Jennings had by this time reached the top of the stairs, but at this home question, she paused to look back at him. "Haven't I just said? We—*you*, that is—are going to steal a march on Sir Valerian."

Theo could find nothing to object to in this plan, although its details were unclear. He followed Mrs. Jennings up the stairs and down the corridor to her room, on the opposite end of the house as his own. He caught up with her only to find her standing before the wardrobe. Having flung open its double doors, she stared with apparent bewilderment at the collection of outmoded finery within.

"Now, where did I put it? Oh, yes! I remember."

She spun away from the wardrobe with the agility of a woman half her age, then dropped to her knees before the bed. Theo watched in some confusion as her entire upper half disappeared beneath the bedframe. Little by little she re-appeared—torso, shoulders, and, finally, her head—dragging in her arms a large pasteboard box.

"Here, let me get that," Theo said quickly, realizing her intention. "Do you want it on the bed?"

She surrendered her burden gratefully. "So very kind— so very like your poor mother—yes, that will be fine."

Theo set the box on the bed, and Mrs. Jennings lifted the lid almost lovingly. The sharp scent of camphor filled the room as she pushed aside layers of yellowed muslin until, finally, she found what she sought. There inside the box lay a complete set of formal clothing suitable for a gentleman: a double-breasted tailcoat of dark blue Bath superfine, black stockinette pantaloons, and a dark red waistcoat of silk brocade, along with a fine cambric shirt, white silk stockings, kid leather pumps with tarnished silver buckles, and a—

"The cravat," Theo said irrelevantly, staring in rapt

wonder at the stiff length of linen, rolled rather than folded in order to preserve its shape. "It's starched."

"It was my son's." The gentle caress with which her arthritic hands stroked the collar of the coat gave Theo to understand that it was the entire ensemble, not merely the cravat, that had belonged to her son. "He was to have been married in it."

"What happened?"

"He fell ill. The wedding was postponed, and then postponed again. When his health continued to decline, he released Miss—well, never mind her name, for she has changed it since then. Suffice it to say that he released her from the engagement, and after protesting that she had no desire to be released, she finally returned his ring." Mrs. Jennings tugged a lace-trimmed handkerchief from her sleeve and dabbed at her eyes. "On the day we buried him, the announcement of her marriage was published in the *Morning Post*. I was thankful he did not live to learn of it."

"I'm very sorry," Theo said, and meant it. "But what— why—?"

She gave a determined sniff and tucked the handkerchief back into her sleeve. "It deserves a happier fate than to remain hidden beneath my bed, a memorial to heartbreak and loss. It is perhaps a bit out of date, but gentlemen's fashions haven't changed so very much, have they? And we can't have you courting Daphne looking like a common laborer."

"I—I don't know how to thank you," stammered Theo.

"You can thank me by preventing Daphne from marrying that coxcomb, Sir Valerian. She deserves to be a duchess, and he—" She gave a disdainful sniff. "He would turn his own mother out into the street if he thought he could gain from it. I knew his father, and he was just such a one, too."

"Mrs. Jennings, have you told anyone? About who I am?"

"Good heavens, what sort of gabby do you take me for? Whatever you're about, you must have your reasons, and you won't want an old woman meddling in your affairs. When you came down to dinner in that garb, though, I thought you might not object to a bit of assistance."

"Not at all," he assured her with feeling.

"The shoes need a bit of work," she observed, regarding them with disfavor. "We'd best step lively. If you'll run and change your clothes, I'll see if I can't polish them up a bit."

Theo was quick to do as he was bidden, and by the time he padded back to her room on stockinged feet, she had contrived to buff the silver into something resembling a shine. At the sight of him in his borrowed finery, she was obliged to seek recourse once more to the handkerchief in her sleeve.

"They might have been made for you," she said between sniffs. "It's almost like seeing my Edward come back to life."

"Actually, they're a bit loose," Theo confessed, shrugging his shoulders to demonstrate. "He must have been a broad-shouldered fellow, your son."

"Aye, that he was, before the illness took him. A well-built lad he was, and ripe for every kind of lark. He would be delighted to know he was playing some part in your adventures. The shirt has yellowed a bit," she observed, startling Theo once more with her sudden change from sentiment to practicality. "Still, I daresay it won't be noticed in candlelight, and in any case, it's better than what you were wearing before."

"*Much* better," he agreed, stepping into the shoes. These proved to be a little too large, but this problem was easily resolved by stuffing the toes with scraps of silk cut from an old pair of stockings. Having overcome this last obstacle, Theo held out his arm to his benefactress. "I would be honored if you would accept my escort."

This, however, Mrs. Jennings refused to do. "You won't want to dance attendance on me when there's Daphne waiting. Then, too, I would rather be alone tonight with my memories. Seeing you wearing his clothes brings him back to me, you know, in a way nothing has in a very long time."

For a long moment, Theo shifted his weight awkwardly from one foot to the other, then bent and kissed her on the cheek. "In that case, please accept my sincerest thanks—and thank Edward, too, for the use of his clothes. I assure you, I shall never forget it."

16

I do perceive here a divided duty.
WILLIAM SHAKESPEARE, *Othello*

Daphne had seen the squire's barn many times before; in fact, she had been inside it only a few weeks earlier, having been dispatched by her mother on an errand involving the purchase of a pig whose slaughter would provide the residents of the boardinghouse with carefully rationed bacon and ham throughout the long winter months ahead. Tonight, however, the building had been transformed. Many of its four-legged residents had met with the same fate as the Drinkards' pig, and their salted carcasses now hung in the smoke house. Their more fortunate fellows had been turned out into the pasture for the occasion, and the newly vacated barn had been shoveled out and its floorboards scrubbed until no threat to the ladies' dancing slippers remained. Lanterns had been hung from the rafters to provide lighting, and a long table set up against one wall groaned under the weight of food and drink provided by Sir Valerian for his guests. Nor had he spared any expense on musicians; rather than old Mr. Barnhill sawing away on his fiddle, as was the usual musical offering at the infrequent local assemblies held at the Red Lion, Sir Valerian had insisted upon sending to Manchester, and fully half a dozen musicians now occupied a makeshift dais at the far end of the barn.

In fact, the matter of dance was one which had caused her mother considerable mental exercise, Daphne recalled, stealing yet another futile glance at the door through which, surely, Mr. Tisdale must enter at any moment. Only a few of Sir Valerian's guests would have enjoyed the tutelage of a dancing master, and yet it would be a very poor hostess who would allow the untutored majority to languish against the wall watching their betters enjoying themselves. The Sir Roger de Coverley had been an easy choice; as it was more than a hundred years old, most of the persons present would have at least a passing familiarity with it, while as for those benighted souls who had not, well, its movements were so simple and so repetitive that one might learn it merely by watching those couples who went down the dance ahead of them. Likewise any contredanse, most of which were based on earlier folk dances, might be enjoyed by the lower classes, although their efforts would not have passed muster in even the most egalitarian of London ballrooms.

The waltz was another matter entirely. To be sure, no London ball would be complete without the fashionable German dance—at least, so said Kitty Morecombe, whose recollections of her own London Seasons never failed to spark a most unworthy sense of envy in Daphne's breast even as she tried (not entirely successfully) to convince herself that Kitty did not mean to gloat. But this was no London ball—not by a long chalk—and most of those present at Sir Valerian's fête would have had no opportunity to learn the steps. Even Daphne, whose own dancing-master had praised the grace with which she executed the figures, had never had an opportunity to demonstrate her skills in public. Still, the prospect of seeing her daughter twirling about the room in Sir Valerian's embrace had worked strongly upon Mrs. Drinkard's mind, and she had finally determined that one— but *only* one—waltz would be played. It was this dance that Daphne had promised to Mr. Tisdale.

Now, however, as she performed the steps of the Scottish reel with Sir Valerian, she wondered if the eagerly anticipated dance would come and go before Mr. Tisdale had even put in an appearance. She could not imagine what might be keeping him so long; she had thought he would be following them immediately after dinner, and although they had been driven to the fête while he would be obliged to travel the distance on foot, surely it could not take so very—

This worrisome train of thought was interrupted when a slight stirring near the door attracted her attention. She missed a step and barreled into Sir Valerian's chest.

"Miss Drinkard?" He caught her arms to steady her. "Are you all right?"

She raised glowing eyes to his. "Oh, yes! I'm quite all right. I—I beg your pardon. I'm not usually so clumsy. I can't—I can't think what came over me."

He glanced in the direction where her attention had been fixed at the time of her stumble, and saw a golden-haired stranger clad in evening attire. No, not a stranger; his newly appointed personal secretary, dressed in garments that, besides being fully two decades out of date, had obviously been made for someone else.

"Oh?" Sir Valerian regarded Daphne with one eyebrow lifted. "Can you not?"

It was perhaps fortunate that the movements of the dance required them to separate and return to their places in the line, for Daphne could think of nothing to say in response to this home question. She turned with positive relief to the squire, diagonally opposite her, with whom she must now take a turn, and by the time the dance brought her back to Sir Valerian, she had had time to compose herself. Still, an eternity seemed to pass before the violins ground to a halt and Sir Valerian escorted her back to her mother.

"What a handsome couple you made!" exclaimed Mrs. Drinkard after he had thanked her for the dance and taken himself off to solicit the vicar's daughter for the next set. "What, pray, did he say to bring such a blush to your cheeks?"

"Why—why nothing, Mama. If I was blushing, it was because I had failed to mind my steps, with disastrous results. Did you not see me crash into the poor man? If I was blushing, it was because I was ready to sink with mortification!"

Mrs. Drinkard gave her a rapturous look. "And oh!—the way he caught you in his arms! It was exceedingly clever of you, my dear. But mind, I think you a very sly minx!"

"But—I didn't—"

"Depend upon it, we shall have you betrothed by midnight!"

"I should not presume—" Daphne protested, resolving nevertheless to give Sir Valerian a wide berth until that hour, just in case. Her demurrals were cut short as the violins began a song in three-quarter time, and in the next instant *he* was there.

"I've come to claim my waltz, Miss Drinkard," Theo said, bowing over her hand. "I hope you haven't forgotten."

"N-no, indeed! Mama, if you will excuse me—"

Her mother looked less than pleased at this latest development, but as it would have been shockingly rag-mannered for Daphne to have danced twice in succession with the same partner, even had Sir Valerian solicited her hand for the waltz, there was little she could do but nod her consent and trust that the sight of Daphne in the arms of his secretary would spur that parliamentary hopeful to declare himself without further delay.

As for Daphne, Sir Valerian occupied no more place in her thoughts than he did in her affections. "You are very late, Mr. Tisdale," she chided Theo as he led her onto the floor. "I had almost given you up."

"And miss my waltz? Never!" he declared. "But there was a little matter of dress to attend to. It took longer than I intended."

"It was time well spent, for you look very fine," she assured him.

"Twenty years out of date, at the very least," he confessed, grinning ruefully at her. "Fortunately for me, gentlemen's fashions don't change so very quickly."

Daphne could not fail to read into this remark an

unflattering awareness of her own three-year-old gown. "So is mine out of date. At least, Kitty—Lady Dandridge, I should say, who was my particular friend before she went to London and married Lord Dandridge—she says no one is wearing gowns with only one flounce around the hem anymore."

"I shouldn't like to disparage your friends, but she sounds to me like a spiteful old cat," he said, his arm tightening protectively about her waist. "And even if it were true, well, one look at you in that gown would have every lady in London ripping the excess flounces from her dresses, for they would all look fussy by comparison."

She looked up at him with an expression combining skepticism and playfulness. "I don't believe you for one minute, but it's very kind of you to say so."

"Perfectly true," he insisted. "Why, my sister would agree, and she—" He broke off abruptly.

" 'She'?" Daphne prompted.

"She knows more about fashion than any female I know," he concluded lamely.

Daphne was certain that was not what he had intended to say, but chose not to press him. "I didn't know you had a sister. You've never said anything about your family before."

Theo shrugged. "There's not much to tell. I don't remember much about my mother, for she died while I was still in the nursery. My father died quite—quite recently. Then there's my sister and her husband and children."

Daphne was more interested in the late Mr. Tisdale. "Did your father leave debts too, then?" she asked in ready sympathy. "Is that why you're working in the mill?"

Theo nodded. "You—you might say so."

"But what of your sister's husband? Can he do nothing to help you?"

Theo was silent for such a long moment that Daphne began to wonder if he intended to answer at all. "He has tried," he said at last. "In fact, he's done more than I realized at first, but he . . . he . . . he . . ."

His words trailed off, and his gaze became fixed on something over her shoulder. Daphne glanced around and saw two or three of the mill workers congregated near the door, their heads together in hushed conversation. She had not noticed before, but the crowd had thinned considerably. All of what her mother termed the more respectable guests remained, but many of the mill workers had apparently found the festivities not to their liking and had left early. Even as her brain registered this observation, the numbers decreased by three; the little group near the door ended their conversation with nods of agreement and slipped outside as a body.

"I—I'm very sorry, Miss Drinkard, but—but I have to go," Theo stammered. His hand fell from her waist, leaving her bereft and just a bit chilly where the warmth of his skin had penetrated the folds of satin. "Let me take you back to your mother."

"Mr. Tisdale, what is wrong?" Daphne asked, struggling to keep up as he took her arm and practically frog-marched her off the floor.

"I don't know, exactly. Possibly nothing."

"But you don't think so," she said, regarding him keenly.

"No, I don't think so. But I have to find out."

"Then I'll come with you."

He shook his head. "If I'm right and some mischief is afoot, I'd rather you weren't mixed up in it."

"If, as you say, some mischief is afoot, it would appear half the village is 'mixed up in it,' " she pointed out, with a sweeping gesture that took in the half-empty barn. "What's more, I'm afraid I might be mixed up in it in any case. This concerns the meetings Mama has allowed Sir Valerian to hold in our house, doesn't it?"

He looked down into her wide, troubled eyes, and could not bring himself to put her off with reassuring half-truths. "Yes, I'm afraid so."

"Then surely I have some right to know!"

In fact, it would be her mother, rather than Daphne, who had a right to know if some skullduggery had been taking place beneath her own roof. But Theo, observing Mrs. Drinkard in animated conversation with the squire's wife, had no great confidence in that lady's discretion—if, in fact, he could make her believe anything ill of Sir Valerian at all. She had not yet noticed her daughter's departure from the dance floor, but she might look their way at any minute, and when she did—

"All right," Theo said. "Come with me. But if anyone should ask, you felt faint from the heat, and I merely took you outside for a breath of fresh air."

He did not wait for her agreement, but steered her out the ill-fitting back door of the barn, wincing at the screech of the rusty hinges. It took a moment for their eyes to adjust to the dark, but there was a full moon, and it was not difficult to tell where the men had gone, for a faint orange glow showed just over a rise in the meadow. Theo put a finger to his lips to silence the questions that trembled on the tip of her tongue, then took her hand and picked his way across the meadow in the dark. As they crested the ridge, he saw more than fifty men, all bearing flaming torches and armed with a hodgepodge of farm implements. From his vantage point, Theo could see pitchforks, shovels, pickaxes, and even something that might have been a cricket bat silhouetted against the flickering orange light.

As he stared in mounting horror, a harsh voice that could only have belonged to Abel Wilkins bellowed, "Are you with me?"

The assembled men shouted their assent.

"To the mill, then!"

"To the mill!" echoed the men, and the torches bobbed crazily against the night sky as the group set out toward the road that led to the village and the cotton mill beyond.

"Good God!" Theo stared down at Daphne, his eyes glittering in the feeble light. "They're marching on the mill! I've got to stop them!"

She clung to his sleeve. "No! What can you possibly do against fifty armed men?"

"I don't know," he said, setting his jaw, "but I have to do something."

"Very well, then," she said resolutely. "I'm coming with you."

"You, my girl, are getting out of here! Ethan Brundy's house has a safe room. He had it put in when the house was built, for just such an emergency." He glanced toward the barn and the field beyond. "It's not very far if you cut across the pasture."

"And I suppose the butler will invite me in and usher me to the safe room with no questions asked!"

"Tell him the Duke of Reddington said he was to let you stay there until further notice."

"*The Duke of—*" she echoed incredulously. "The duke might have something to say about that!"

"Daphne, I don't have time to argue the matter with you! Just *go!*"

He called me Daphne. Her heart rejoiced, but she hadn't the luxury of savoring the sound of her name on his lips. "Mr. Tisdale—Theo—you will be careful, won't you?"

Theo had already begun to turn away, but at this entreaty he stopped, seized her by the arms, and kissed her swift and hard on the mouth. The kiss was over almost as soon as it began, but when he would have released her, she flung her arms about his neck and kissed him back with all the love and passion and fear she could never put into words. But if she had thought to deter him from the path he was set on, she was doomed to disappointment. All too soon, he broke the kiss and set her firmly at arm's length.

"Now, go," he said a bit breathlessly, putting a hand to the small of her back and giving her a little nudge in the direction of the barn.

It made her want to cry, the fact that the kiss she had so longed for had come under such circumstances, and the knowledge that he might not live long enough to kiss her again. But he was urging her to go, and if she could do nothing else to help him, she could at least obey him in this. She dared not look back for fear her feelings would betray her, but picked up her skirts and ran toward the barn, avoiding the wide double doors that allowed the light within to spill out, exposing her flight to anyone who might happen to glance that way. Instead, she made for the rear of the building, then circled the far corner—

And ran into Sir Valerian Wadsworth with sufficient force to knock the breath from her body.

"My dear Miss Drinkard!" he exclaimed, taking her by the shoulders to steady her. His hand was warm on her bare skin, and she realized her gown had slipped from one shoulder in her mad flight. "Where have you been? Your mother has been greatly disturbed by your absence, and could not be easy until I offered to go in search of you."

Recalling Theo's instructions, she stammered in between gulps of air, "I was feeling faint—stepped outside—Mr. Tisdale—fresh air—"

"I see," he said smoothly, looking past her to the meadow beyond. "But where is Mr. Tisdale now?"

"He is—gone. He—" *He's gone to confront fifty angry men armed with torches and pitchforks, all on his own.* No, surely the time for dissembling was past. "Sir Valerian, the workers are marching on the mill. He's gone to—to try and stop them. Please, you must help him! Perhaps they will listen to you."

He drew her hand through the curve of his arm and patted it soothingly. "I daresay he must have misunderstood, and the men have merely gone in search of stronger drink than anything on offer tonight. Pray do not trouble yourself! Let me take you back inside. Will you not allow me the honor of partnering you for the next set? I believe it will be forming soon."

"I assure you, there can be no mistake! We should—we *must* do something!"

His voice hardened, and the hand covering hers tightened painfully. "If it is truly as you say, Miss Drinkard, then you would do well to stay out of matters that don't concern you."

Startled and a bit frightened by the change in his tone, she looked up at him. The obsequious manner he had always adopted toward her was gone. The lines about his mouth were cast into strong relief by the moonlight, and his eyes glittered, cruel and utterly ruthless.

"It was you," she said, stunned by the realization. "That's what the meetings were about. You incited the mill workers to riot."

"I?" His eyebrows rose in an exaggerated indication of surprise. "I've been here all evening, entertaining my guests. You should know, for you danced with me yourself."

"Yes, I did, didn't I?" Her voice held more conviction now. "I must be sure to bathe when I return home. Suddenly I feel dirty."

He released her hand, but only long enough to grab her arm and pull her to him, so close that they stood nearly nose to nose. "Perhaps you *feel* dirty because you *are* dirty. Let me remind you that the meetings you so deplore were held beneath your mother's roof, with her full cooperation and your own assistance. You're in this up to your pretty neck, my dear, and if I go down, I won't hesitate to take you and your ambitious mother with me. Now, you're going back inside with me, do you understand? You're going to dance with me, and you're going to like it."

You're going to like it . . . The words rang in her head, warning her, reminding her of—what? *You're going to like it . . . Like it . . . Like . . . The next time a man does something you don't like . . .*

Oh, Theo, she thought, *I hope you're right.* She took a deep breath, then snatched up her skirts with her free hand and drove her knee into Sir Valerian's groin with all the force she could muster.

The results astounded her. Sir Valerian dropped to his knees with a groan of agony, the hands that had gripped her now cupped protectively over the site of the assault. Forgetting, at least for a moment, the need for haste, Daphne stared down in rapt wonder at what she had wrought.

"It works!"

At the sound of her voice, Sir Valerian looked up, his face turning quite purple as he unleashed upon her a tirade in which he castigated her as a Jezebel, among other things, most of which were unsuitable for mixed company, and several of which she had never even heard before. Daphne had no time to waste on him. She spun away and took herself off in the direction of the Brundy residence as quickly as the moonlit night, the uneven ground, and the thin dancing slippers on her feet would allow.

17

*May men say, "He is far greater than his father,"
when he returns from battle.*
HOMER, *The Iliad*

The band of rioting workers appeared to be heading for the road that led to the mill, so Theo set out across the fields in the same direction, hoping to reach it ahead of them. Exactly what he would do when he got there was unclear; still, it behooved him to do *something*. He could only hope some plan of action would have presented itself to him when the time came.

He reached the mill to find it dark and quiet. Stepping up to the nearest window, he cupped his hands about his eyes, pressed his nose to the glass, and peered inside. Moonlight shining on the rows of machines cast weird shadows onto the sanded planks of the floor, but there was no sign of any movement, and no sound. Clearly, he had got there ahead of the mob, in spite of having twice lost his way and once wrenched his ankle by stepping into a rabbit hole. He had not long to wonder at this curious circumstance before a faint orange glow over the hill, accompanied by a murmur of sound like a swarm of angry bees, announced the approach of his adversaries. But surely the glow was brighter than it had been before. Or was it merely an optical illusion, a trick of the moonlight as its source rose higher in the sky?

Then the first of the torches began to crest the hill, and Theo's thudding heart dropped into the region usually occupied by his stomach. What had been surely no more than fifty men had increased to two—three—four times that number. What could any one man do against such an army?

"Buck up, old boy," he admonished himself under his breath. "You were already outnumbered fifty to one. What's a couple hundred more?"

Setting his jaw, he stepped away from the window and positioned himself before the door.

* * *

Lady Helen Brundy, exhausted from three days on the road, leaned her head back against the squabs and attempted, without much success, to sleep. Well-sprung as it undoubtedly was, her husband's traveling carriage was no substitute for the goose down pillow that awaited her at the end of the journey. Her glance rested briefly on the rear-facing seat, where her son lay curled up with his head on his father's lap, and she envied him the easy slumber of the young.

Her husband, correctly interpreting her wistful expression, gave her a look that might have been a caress. "Not much longer now, love."

"No," she concurred, summoning a weary smile.

Her gaze shifted to the window, beyond which familiar

landmarks might occasionally be glimpsed in the light of the carriage's swaying lanterns: a signpost indicating the direction and distance to Manchester; a thatched cottage distinguished, incongruously, by a tiny square window of stained glass; the silver gleam of moonlight on water as they crossed the bridge over the River Medlock. Then another sight, less familiar, met her eyes. She sat up straighter, peering out the window for a closer look at the faint orange glow in the distance.

"Ethan, something is burning. You don't suppose—the house—"

He shifted Willie's limp form and leaned forward, almost pressing his nose to the glass. "It couldn't be the 'ouse; it's not far enough to the north. All the same—"

He rapped sharply on the overhead panel, and ordered the coachman not to spare the horses.

* * *

"Stop right there!" Theo bellowed as soon as the mob was close enough to hear. He took a step forward, out of the shadow of the hulking building at his back, and drew himself up to his full height.

"Lookee here," came a jeering voice Theo had no trouble identifying as Wilkins. "It's Thee-o-dore."

"Step aside, Tisdale," someone else warned him. "You don't want to get hurt."

Theo was in complete agreement with this statement, but held his ground nonetheless.

"We've got no grudge against you, so long as you'll not interfere."

"Are you with us, or not?"

Now they were near enough that he could pick out faces, their features distorted by shadow and flame, but recognizable nevertheless. Perhaps it was nothing more than a trick of the light, but while some of them looked angry and ready to torch the mill at a word from Wilkins, others looked uncomfortable and ill at ease. He decided his best course lay in making his appeal to these.

"I'm with you," he assured them. "I'm with you so much that I've come to urge you not to do anything you'll regret."

Wilkins gave a bark of laughter. "Oh, we won't regret it, although Brundy might. He's had it coming for years."

"Has he? What has he ever done to you?" Theo looked beyond Wilkins to address the group at large. "What has he done to any of you?"

It was the wrong thing to say.

"Living like a king—"

"—that big house of his—"

"—standing for Parliament—"

"Aye, while we sweat and slave for him—"

As Theo listened to their catalog of grievances, it struck him that they were reciting lines they'd learned by rote—learned from Wilkins, he had no doubt, at Sir Valerian's instigation.

"All right, so he's rich," he said, conceding the point. "But can any of you honestly say that he's never 'sweated and slaved' himself?" Seeing them momentarily silenced, Theo pressed his point. "Right after the war, when the price of bread was so high and the cost of cotton plummeted, did he reduce your wages by so much as a farthing? Or let any of you go, so he wouldn't have to pay so many workers? No, he canceled the trip to Paris he was to take with Nell, er, with his family, instead."

Too late, Theo realized they might wonder how he had come by this information. But no, there was an uncomfortable shuffling of feet, and a moment later one of the men—Theo couldn't remember his name—tossed his pickaxe to the ground and took up a position beside him.

"Tisdale is right," he declared.

"Er, you might want to hold onto that," murmured Theo, nodding toward his abandoned weapon. Aloud, he continued to press his point. "What about you, Jack? When you were so sick and couldn't work for a week, did he withhold your pay? Or yours, Gerry, when you were obliged to go to Staffordshire and take care of your mum after your father died?"

There was a further shuffling as first Jack and then Gerry took up positions flanking Theo. *Two hundred to four,* Theo thought. *Things are looking up.*

"Did you never think," Theo went on, inspired to new heights of rhetoric, "that, because he knows what it's like to work in the mill, he might be doing what he can to make sure things are better for all of you? That that's why he wants to stand for Parliament in the first place?"

"Sir Valerian Wadsworth says he'll do more for us than Brundy ever did!" declared Wilkins, unwilling to give up without a fight.

"A man you met, what, two months ago?" Theo scoffed. "And what evidence do you have that he'll do as he says, or even think of you at all, after the election is over? What do any of you really know about him?"

"Sir Valerian is a man of his word!" The reply came, not from Wilkins, but from one of his supporters.

"What? Just because his father was someone important?" challenged the latest in a long line of hereditary dukes. "Surely you know better than that!"

"Why else would he care about helping us, when we can't even vote?"

"Because if you torch the mill, he can point to your actions and tell those who *can* vote that Sir Ethan Brundy can't even keep his own affairs in order, much less the nation's. He's using you—all of you—and you're playing right into his hands."

It was a tactical error. No man liked to be played for a fool, as he had discovered for himself when he'd realized that La Fantasia's supposed affection for him had been no more than her conviction that in him she had found a greenhorn who could be manipulated into making her a duchess. Whatever the difference in their respective births, these men had no less pride than Theo himself. In fact, it might be argued that pride was all they had. In such a case, they would surely cling to it all the more tightly.

"All right," Theo said, raising his hands in mock surrender. "Go ahead and torch the place. But how are you going to feed your families tomorrow morning, or the day after that?"

"This ain't the only mill in the world!" bellowed a harsh voice.

"I've worked a power loom for twenty years," boasted another. "I could find work tomorrow."

"Yes, working fifteen-hour days," agreed Theo, nodding in agreement. "That's assuming, of course, that any mill owner is willing to take a chance on a man who'd just burned his previous place of employment to the ground."

"Who's to know?" retorted Wilkins. "Unless you intend to talk." He lowered his weapon, but any relief Theo might have felt was negated by the realization that the knife in the man's hand was now aimed directly at his chest.

"It's a country village," Theo pointed out, determinedly ignoring the sick feeling in the pit of his stomach. "Can you— any of you—honestly believe it would remain a secret for long? Do you think no one has noticed that you've all slipped away from the party, and if the mill is burned to the ground by morning, no one is going to put two and two together?"

"That's enough!" bellowed Wilkins. He rushed at Theo, only to be brought up short in mid-stride by the last voice he had ever expected to hear.

"What the devil's going on 'ere?"

Theo had never heard his brother-in-law speak in that particular tone of voice, and hoped to God never to be on the receiving end of it. Still, at that moment it was the most beautiful sound he had ever heard.

"Ethan!" Theo let out a sigh of relief. "Thank God!"

Sir Ethan paid him not the slightest heed, but addressed himself to his rebellious workers. "Well?"

There was a moment of rather abashed silence, then everyone seemed to be talking at once.

"Wilkins said—"

"Sir Valerian—"

"—said we deserved—"

"—told us we ought to—"

"Oh, so it's Sir Valerian, is it?" Sir Ethan remarked knowingly. "That explains a lot."

And then the demurrals began.

"I never wanted to—"

"—always said he was—"

"—seemed a bit shady to me—"

"—I didn't mean to—"

Sir Ethan silenced their protestations with one upraised hand. "Men, it's very late and I've been traveling for three days. Let's all go 'ome and get some sleep, and I'll 'ear you out in the morning. Let's say, eight o'clock."

And just that simply, it was over. With much shuffling of feet and many shamefaced glances, the men took themselves off, lowering their makeshift weapons as if wondering how such things had ever come to be in their hands.

"I'm deuced glad to see you, Ethan," Theo said as soon as they were alone. "I'm not sure I could have held them off much longer. Truth to tell, I'd decided my letter must have gone amiss."

"Your letter?" echoed Sir Ethan, regarding his young kinsman with an arrested expression.

"I sent you a letter telling you that Wilkins was bullying the workers and that I was afraid some kind of trouble was in the wind. When you never came, I thought you must not have received it."

Now it was the mill owner's turn to look sheepish. "Oh, I received it, all right. I burned it without ever opening it. I'm sorry; I recognized your 'andwriting, and thought you were begging me to let you leave the mill."

"Oh, I don't doubt I would have, if I'd thought it would do the least good," Theo confessed, grinning. "But I was never one to fling my cap after lost causes."

"And yet you faced down an angry mob alone and unarmed. That sounds like a lost cause to me."

"Don't think it was by choice! It's just that, well, I had to do something, so—" He broke off, shrugging.

"Still, I stand in your debt, Theo. You saved the mill, and I won't soon forget it. But if we're to talk of letters, what of my letter to you? I wrote to tell you probate's been granted. You're free to claim your in'eritance anytime you please."

"Yes, it came three days ago. But by that time, I'd discovered something ugly was in the wind and, well, I couldn't leave with things in such a state."

Sir Ethan gave him a long, searching look. "I think per'aps you'll make a duke, after all."

Theo suddenly recalled something else his brother-in-law ought to know. "Oh, I should tell you—at the start of the trouble, I sent Daphne—Miss Drinkard, that is—to your house, to the safe room." He set his jaw. "And you might as well know that I intend to marry her."

"Yes, your grace," replied Ethan with a meekness in his manner that was utterly belied by the twinkle in his eye. "And is there anything else you intend to do?"

Theo considered the matter. "I think—I think I should

like to take up my seat in the House of Lords. I know it's expensive—I daresay that's why Papa never bothered with it—but I think I should like to be a voice for men like Ben and Tom and Davy—men who don't have a voice of their own. That is, I'd like to try," he added with unaccustomed shyness, "if you think I can."

Sir Ethan clapped a hand to his shoulder. "I not only think you can; I think you'll do very well, Reddington."

"Reddington," echoed Theo with a self-conscious little laugh. "You never called me that before."

"You never acted like it before," said Sir Ethan, and together they left the mill, dark and peaceful in the moonlight.

* * *

For Daphne, it was the most frightening, most glorious, most bewildering night of her life. To be sure, the butler at the Brundy residence had seemed a bit taken aback by the appearance of a young lady clad in evening attire and requesting to be shown to the safe room, but at the mention of the Duke of Reddington, any misgivings he might have harbored were apparently banished. He ushered her at once to a small windowless chamber comfortably furnished with everything one might need for a protracted stay, but when he expressed his intention of bringing her some light refreshment, she felt compelled to protest.

"Oh, no, pray do not! That is, I should not want to put you to any trouble."

Evers bestowed an avuncular smile upon her and assured her (quite truthfully, as it was his employers' larder, and not his own, which would be diminished) that it was no trouble at all.

Daphne was surprised to discover that, her fear for Theo's safety notwithstanding, she was in fact quite famished; she had eaten very little at the fête, so intent had she been on watching the door for his arrival. And so, when Evers arrived a short time later with the tea tray, she was emboldened to ask him if she might perhaps have some bread and butter.

"Of course, miss, if you have no objection to sharing the servants' board. I regret that Lady Helen is at present in London, and so cannot receive you."

But in this, it soon proved, he was mistaken. For Daphne had hardly finished spreading her second slice of coarse brown bread with creamy butter and orange marmalade when the door to the safe room opened and Lady Helen Brundy herself entered the room.

"Good evening, Miss Drinkard," she said, extending one gloved hand. "I'm sorry you have been left to cool your heels all alone for so long. I should have come to you as soon as Evers informed me that you were here, but my naughty son William, having slept most of the way from Stockport, must needs decide it is now time to play! But tell me, how may I be of service to you?"

Daphne suddenly found herself tongue-tied. Lady Helen Brundy was scarcely more than five years older than she was herself, but she possessed a forcefulness of character and an elegance of person that Daphne found daunting. "I—that is— Mr. Tisdale—I mean—I was told to say that the Duke of Reddington requested that I be allowed to stay in your safe room until further notice." This, at least, had the virtue of being true, so far as it went. "There was trouble at the mill, you see, and he—he—"

"Yes, we saw the flames from the road," Lady Helen said. "But—"

"Flames?" Daphne seized upon the word. "They did it, then? They set the mill afire?" In fact, her concern was less for the mill than it was for the gallant Mr. Tisdale, but if the mob had succeeded in torching the mill, it must surely bode very ill for the one man who had tried to stop them.

Lady Helen hastened to reassure her. "No, at least not—but—'Mr. Tisdale,' you say?"

"H-he was going to stop them. He—"

She broke off as the door swung open. She had been prepared to make some excuse for being there uninvited (although, in truth, these sounded feeble even to her own mind), but Sir Ethan Brundy appeared utterly unperturbed by her presence. In fact, he acknowledged her with only the briefest of nods before addressing himself to his wife.

"A word with you, 'elen."

"Of course." Lady Helen excused herself to Daphne, then followed her husband from the room. He closed the door behind her, leaving Daphne to wait in a silence so complete as to be oppressive; one of the unique features of this room, it appeared, was that it blocked all sound. The return of her host and hostess a few minutes later did little enough to enlighten her. Lady Helen apologized profusely for being what she termed "shockingly rag-mannered," and after assuring Daphne that the trouble at the mill had proven to be nothing more than a storm in a teacup, expressed her intention of accompanying her husband in escorting Daphne home. "For," she concluded, "you will not want to muss your pretty gown by walking back across the fields. Tell me, is it new?"

In some bewilderment, Daphne allowed herself to be led from the house and handed up into the carriage by Sir Ethan himself. Alas, her intention of telling Theo of the night's adventures, and hearing an account of his own doings, suffered a severe check.

For when she returned to the boardinghouse, she was met with the news that Mr. Tisdale had paid his shot, packed his bags, and taken his leave.

18

Love is not love
Which alters when it alteration finds.
WILLIAM SHAKESPEARE, *Sonnet 116*

It had been Theo's intention to return to London only long enough to provide himself with a suitable wardrobe and arrange for a barber to cut his hair before returning to make Daphne an offer in form. Alas, he had failed to take into account the effect his sudden disappearance, protracted absence, and unexpected return would have upon his cronies. He was obliged to agree to not one, but several evenings spent at White's in the company of these sprigs of the nobility, where he stunned his audience by giving an account of his employment at the mill. He attributed this to a wager, as his brother-in-law had suggested, but could not help thinking, even as he did so, how shallow and contemptible it sounded. His friends were so skeptical of this claim that he was obliged to remove his gloves and offer up his hands as proof— although these were, in fact, much improved over the state in which Daphne had found them, his valet having subjected them to a strict regimen of Warren's Milk of Roses, aloe, and Denmark Lotion.

He had then taken the time to write to his steward, authorizing Alfred to see to the re-thatching of any of his tenants' cottages whose roofs might stand in need of it before the winter set in, as well as putting in motion any advance preparations necessary for the draining of the south field the following spring. He also asked, as a personal favor (and one which, although he could not know it, caused the longsuffering steward to shed tears of joy), if Alfred would oblige him by looking in on the men who worked his tin mines and addressing any issues which, in the steward's opinion, might be considered urgent, until such time as the duke could visit these holdings for himself.

He then went to his bank, where most of the good jewelry had been kept in a safety-deposit box since the death of his mother, for the Reddington betrothal ring. Mr. George Dorrien (the same man who, not so very long ago, had denied Theo's request for an advance on his inheritance) was on this occasion all eagerness to serve him, even going so far as to retrieve the desired piece with his own hands and to deliver it to his noble client in person, all in the futile hope of gleaning some clue as to the identity of the lady upon whom it was to be bestowed.

The ring, Theo knew, was a band of chased gold set with a single pear-shaped peridot, designed early in the previous century by a romantically-minded duke as a tribute to the leaf-green eyes of his chosen bride, a lady who had then demonstrated her gratitude by bequeathing this striking physical characteristic to several generations of descendants. In fact, this tidbit of family history had been recounted to Theo numerous times over the years, and all the more so after he had reached the age at which he might begin to look about for a bride of his own; what he had *not* been told was that, having been locked away for almost twenty years, the piece was now sadly in need of cleaning. This being the case, he was obliged to bestow it first upon Mr. John Bridge of the fashionable jewelers Rundell and Bridge, thus delaying his return to Lancashire still further.

What with one thing and another, fully two weeks had passed before Theo knocked once more on the door of the boardinghouse and requested a private audience with Mrs. Drinkard. His former landlady—who, in truth, had not been at all sorry to see him go—received him in her husband's study with a marked lack of enthusiasm, having suspected (quite correctly) that her daughter's failure to bring Sir Valerian up to scratch might be laid at his door. Some quarter of an hour later, she emerged from the interview stunned and reeling, and commanded the kitchen boy to go in search of Daphne and tell her the Duke of Reddington was desirous of a word with her. This lad looked up at his mistress, saw her flushed countenance and the bewildered (and bewildering) look in her eyes, and set out at a run.

He found her at once, for the entire household knew that Miss Daphne had taken to spending her leisure hours standing solitary guard over the foot bridge, leaning against its stone parapet and dropping flower petals one by one into the water below. It was commonly supposed (by all except her fond parent) that Sir Valerian was responsible for Miss Daphne's sudden inertia, his abrupt departure from the vicinity having destroyed the poor girl's last hope of matrimony.

In fact, the rare occasions when Sir Valerian crossed Daphne's mind were the only thoughts capable of bringing a smile to her face. For she could not help picturing the aspiring Member of Parliament as she had last seen him, cowering on his knees and turning purple in the face, all because of the swift and simple movement Theo Tisdale had taught her. And just as suddenly, her smiles would give way to tears. She would never see him again, never be able to tell him of this exchange or how very successful his lessons had proven.

I like mushrooms . . . They'd been standing in this very spot when he had spoken those words, and she had interpreted that simple statement as so much more. It had seemed a declaration, of sorts, and she had treasured it as such. But now it appeared that Mr. Tisdale had never intended it that way. No, he'd only been being kind, only trying to comfort her after Kitty Dandridge had snubbed her at church. As she, like a sentimental fool, had been so desperate for love that she had pinned all her romantic hopes on nothing more than a young man's expression of fondness for edible fungi.

I wish he had never come, she thought with sudden fierceness, flinging the denuded flower stem into the water whence it disappeared beneath the bridge, swept downstream on its long journey to the sea. She wished she might go with it and escape the recollection of her own folly. *I wish I had never met him.*

But even as her brain formed the thought, she knew it for

a lie. The few weeks he had lived at the boardinghouse had been the happiest of her life, a brief glimpse of sunshine in an otherwise dull and gray existence. It was not his fault that the dull now seemed so much duller, the gray so very much grayer. She would treasure the memory of those golden days in her heart, and someday, when she was an old maid and a generation of villagers yet unborn would point to her and whisper pityingly behind their hands that "They say she was once a beauty, you know," he would still be there, forever young, forever golden. Forever hers.

"Miss Daphne! Miss Daphne!" The kitchen boy's breathless cries interrupted her thoughts, and she dabbed her eyes with the corner of her apron.

"Yes, Timmy? What is it?"

"Your ma wants you. She says the"—he screwed up his face in concentration, trying to remember the name—"the Duke of Reddington wants a word with you."

"*The Duke of*—" she echoed, turning quite pale. "Are you quite certain that was the name?"

His head bobbed up and down emphatically. "I'm certain sure. I memorized it special."

Of course that was the name, she chided herself. *How many other dukes are likely to turn up inquiring after you?*

"I beg your pardon, Timmy; of course you did. Run ahead and tell Mama and the duke" —her voice shook slightly on the word— "that I shall be there directly."

As soon as the boy had gone, she stripped off her apron and draped it over the parapet, then pinched her cheeks to give them color and put a hand to her hair to make sure her chignon was still reasonably intact. Clearly, the dance was done and it was now time to pay the piper.

Surely it could not be so very bad, she told herself. The Brundys had not been angry at her entering their house under false pretenses; on the contrary, when she had seen them at church the following Sunday, Lady Helen Brundy had been all that was amiable, even expressing her hope that Daphne and her mother would come to tea one day. It would not have done, of course. Quite aside from the fact that the endless litany of chores left the Drinkard ladies with no time for social niceties, her mother was too conscious of their precarious position in society to jeopardize it by fraternizing with a mill owner, no matter how wealthy he might be. Still, if the Brundys were not offended by her gaining access to their home under false pretenses, then surely the duke could not be so very displeased at having unwittingly lent his name to the cause.

"Oh, my dearest girl!" cried her mother, meeting her with open arms and enveloping her in a slightly floury (for it was baking day) embrace. "Never in my wildest dreams did I ever—but you must not keep his grace waiting. I've put him in your father's study. You must go to him at once!"

"Yes, Mama," said Daphne in a hollow voice, noting her mother's brimming eyes with a growing sense of dread. Apparently the duke was beyond displeased, beyond even offended. He must be livid, if he had brought her mother to such a state; under less dire circumstances, Mama would be over the moon at having a duke beneath her roof. With a last, nervous pat to her hair, Daphne crossed the hall to the study, then took a deep breath, opened the door, and stepped inside.

The sight that met her eyes deprived her of speech. There stood Mr. Tisdale, the light from the tall windows turning his hair to gold. Of the Duke of Reddington there was no sign; it seemed somehow absurd to think that such a personage might have felt the need to excuse himself to the necessary, but even dukes were human, Daphne supposed. In any case, his absence allowed her a moment alone with Theo. Strangely, she was no longer afraid, now that she did not have to face the duke's wrath alone.

"Theo!" she exclaimed in an undervoice, softly closing the door behind her. "The duke—does he know it was you who—"

"No—that is—yes, he—he knew it all along." He crossed the room to where she still stood just inside the door. "In fact, the Duke of Reddington is—well—he's me."

Daphne could only stare at him as the significance of these simple words became clear. Her stunned brain began to register the details she had missed before in the shock and, yes, joy of seeing him again: the double-breasted tailcoat of Bath superfine; the striped satin waistcoat; the tasseled Hessian boots, polished to such a sheen that they might have served, in a pinch, for a looking glass. Even his golden curls, which she *had* noticed, were no longer entirely familiar, having been fashionably cropped and brushed until they shone.

In short, he looked every inch a duke, while she was dusted with flour and dressed in her oldest gown, and she had believed she'd found in him a kindred spirit whose circumstances were no better than her own, while all the time he had been—he had been—

The next time a man does something you don't like . . .

She snatched up her flour-sprinkled skirts and jerked her knee up, just as he had once taught her in this very room.

Theo jumped out of range with a yelp. "Daphne, you little hellcat! What the—"

"How dare you?" she demanded, hopping after him on one foot while she tried without success to make contact with her other knee. "How dare you come here and—and laugh at me—at all of us—"

"I never laughed at you," he assured her gently, taking her by the shoulders but holding her at arm's length, just in case. "How could I?"

"Still, you might have told me," she said, wiping away angry tears with her sleeve. "I told you all about Papa, and about how things stood with Mama and me, but still you said nothing."

"But I did," he insisted. "I told you I was a gentleman who'd temporarily fallen on hard times."

"You admitted it after I guessed it on my own," she retorted. "It's not at all the same thing."

"But—but, dash it," Theo protested. "After hearing what happened to you, what your father had done, how could I look you in the face after admitting that I'd been no better? D'you think I was proud of the fact that I'd managed to run myself to grass within days of coming into the title?"

She blinked at him. "You did? But—*how?*"

He shoved his hand through his hair, disarranging the

modish curls. "I've asked myself the same question a hundred times. Part of it—most of it, I suppose—was cowardice, pure and simple."

"*Cowardice?*" Daphne echoed, picturing once more the image of Theo going off to face an angry mob without so much as a stout stick to defend himself. "You are the bravest man I've ever known! What you did at the mill that night—"

"Oh, *that*," he said, dismissing it with an impatient gesture. "That wasn't bravery; it was simple necessity. I had to do something, and so—but this was different. Suddenly all the responsibility of the dukedom was mine, and there would be no more running to Papa to extricate me when I found myself in difficulties. Then, too, I had a longstanding pact with some of my old friends from Oxford days, to celebrate whenever one of us came unto his title—all at the new peer's expense, of course—and I had to hold up my end of the bargain. We played cards at White's, and I lost—one always does, when one most needs to win. Finally, there was a—a woman who expected me to marry her, although I never gave her the least reason to think—anyway, it was necessary to—well, to buy her off. Compensation for breaking her heart, she said, although I could give you another name for it."

"And this lady found *money* an acceptable substitute for your affections?" Daphne asked, indignant on his behalf.

"To be perfectly honest, it was jewelry, not money. And although she was a woman, she was certainly *not* a lady."

"Oh," Daphne said in a small voice.

"Anyway," Theo continued, "it wasn't until after all this that I discovered I couldn't touch my inheritance until Papa's will had been probated."

"And so you came to work at the mill."

He shook his head. "Not at once. My brother-in-law is my father's executor, and although he said he couldn't legally give me an advance against Papa's estate, he did offer to lend me the money, under one condition: he wouldn't charge any interest on the loan, but I would work at the mill until I could pay it back out of my inheritance." He snapped his fingers in sudden realization. "Dash it! I knew there was something I forgot to do while I was in London!"

"Your brother-in-law," Daphne said thoughtfully. "He must be—"

"Ethan—that is, Sir Ethan Brundy, who owns the mill. His wife, Lady Helen, is my sister."

Of course she is, Daphne thought, recalling the poised beauty with the honey-colored hair—a shade or two darker than her brother's, although the green eyes were the very same. She could only wonder why she hadn't thought of it before.

"It seems rather harsh of him, treating a member of his wife's family in such a way."

"So I thought at the time—and don't think I didn't let him know it! In fact, it wasn't until I'd exhausted all other avenues that I agreed to such a scheme. But looking back, I can see it was all for the best—yes, and I suspect *he* knew it, too, and that was what he was doing all along! I hope to be a better duke—a better *man*—for having known Ben, and Tom, and all the men at the mill. And you and your mother and your boarders, too." He grinned suddenly, and Daphne's heart did strange and wonderful things in response. "Especially Mrs. Jennings. I took her son's wedding clothes back to London with me, and had my valet clean and brush them before bringing them back to her. She knew who I was all along, can you believe it? She had been acquainted with my mother in her youth, and I'm said to bear a strong likeness to her. My mother, that is, not Mrs. Jennings."

"I've always suspected Mrs. Jennings is sharper than she lets on," Daphne said, smiling bravely. Here it was, then, the reason for his unexpected return. It was nothing to do with the Duke of Reddington, nothing to do with *her*, at all. "It was kind of you to have the clothes cleaned for her, and to deliver them yourself. And to—to seek me out to say goodbye. I was worried about you that night, and I—I had wondered, when you left without a word."

She held out her hand to him, but Theo, staring at her in stunned disbelief, made no move to take it. "You can't think I asked to speak privately with you for such a reason as that!"

"Then—what—?"

He did not answer at once, but fumbled in the breast pocket of his elegant coat. Having found what he sought, he withdrew a small velvet box and opened its hinged lid. In one graceful movement, he sank to one knee and offered the box to her. "Daphne Drinkard, will you do me the honor of bestowing upon me your hand in marriage?"

She caught a glimpse of bright green peridots—two in his eyes, and one in the box he held, set in a ring of chased gold—before pressing her hands to her face. "No, Theo— your grace—you must not!"

"Oh? Why mustn't I? And why, for that matter, am I suddenly 'your grace' when I was 'Theo' only a few moments ago? I expect a good reason, mind you, and no missish airs!"

He succeeded in persuading her to uncover her face, but although she choked back a reluctant laugh, she shook her head. "Surely you must see that it was different before—"

"Oh, I'll not argue with you there. It was certainly different—and a deuced sight more uncomfortable! But I can't regret it, for if Ethan hadn't insisted on putting me to work in that curst mill of his, I would very likely never have met you."

"But—but you might marry *anyone!*"

"Believe me, I'm well aware of that." The bitterness in his voice robbed the words of any arrogance. "The Duke of Reddington can have his pick of females eager for him to drop the handkerchief in their direction. And if their matrimonial hopes should be dashed, well, there's no heartbreak so severe that a sufficient outlay of cash won't heal. But you"—he rose to his feet and drew her to him with one arm about her waist while his other hand tipped her chin up, forcing her to look him in the face—"you loved me when I was Mr. Tisdale, a poor gentleman fallen on hard times and forced to earn his bread by working in a cotton mill. At least, I thought you did."

"I did," she whispered, and although he still held her chin captive, her gaze slid away to stare with great intensity at the knot in his liberally starched cravat. "Even when I knew it must break Mama's heart."

"I can assure you that when I asked your mother for

permission to pay my addresses to you, she appeared to be in no immediate danger of heartbreak."

She gave a little gurgle of laughter, considering her mother's reaction to "Mr. Tisdale's" presence in the light of this new revelation. "I can just imagine! But Theo, much as I might want to—much as I *do* want to—I can't marry you. I can't go off and leave Mama to run the boardinghouse all alone!"

"She need not run the boardinghouse at all if she doesn't choose to."

She shook her head. "It is very kind of you, but she would never turn her boarders out. It is only that she doesn't have enough staff as it is, and without me there to help—"

"I only meant that she could live in the dower house, if she wants to be close to you. Surely there's no shortage of impoverished gentlewomen who would welcome a roof over their heads and a reasonably genteel position."

Daphne dimpled at him. "In other words, another mushroom in need of a good wine sauce."

"Just so," he said, grinning back at her. "But if your mother prefers to remain in her own home, you can be sure that she will have all the staff she desires, and enough housekeeping money that she won't have to ration the tea. And although I have no desire to encourage drunkenness, I think I can guarantee that she and her boarders will be able to have more than half a glass of wine a day. I might even be able to promise Mr. Nethercote a glass of port every evening. Although I'd best speak up when I tell him so, or he'll think I'm offering to lance a wart."

"Only Mr. Nethercote?" asked Daphne, confused by the deliberate omission of the boardinghouse's only other male resident. "Not Mr. Nutley?"

"I think Mr. Nutley will be much happier as vicar of a rural parish. The Dukes of Reddington have several modest livings in their gift, one of which is vacant at the moment. I had thought to offer it to him." In a more serious tone, he added, "No one should be punished forever for foolish mistakes they committed when they were young. Do you think, perhaps, that you could forgive me for mine? Daphne, I do love you so."

"Oh, Theo!" Her voice choked on a sob as she flung her arms around him.

"Am I to take that as a 'yes'?" he asked, emerging at last from a kiss that left them both panting and breathless.

"Yes," she confessed shyly. "Only—Theo, I don't know *anything* about being a duchess!"

"I don't know anything about being a duke, either," he admitted with a shrug. "What do you say we figure it out together?"

And so they did.

Epilogue

The gardener Adam and his wife
Smile at the claims of long descent.
ALFRED, LORD TENNYSON, *Lady Clara Vere de Vere*

July 2018
Reddington Hall, Devon

A nd here we have something of a mystery," pronounced the tour guide ("Katherine," according to the name tag pinned to her starched white blouse), her high-heeled shoes clicking against the marble-tiled floor as she crossed the room to indicate a framed piece of needlework hanging over the mantel. "If you look carefully, you can see faint brown flecks in the fabric. Family legend claims that the ninth duke wove the fabric himself, having fallen into financial difficulties and been forced to seek employment at a cotton mill, and that those specks are the places where his fingers bled, he being unaccustomed to physical labor."

Phones came out and cameras snapped, and Jill, an attractive young woman in her mid-twenties with curling brown hair and large, deceptively somber brown eyes, spoke for the group by asking, "But you don't believe it?"

Katherine the Tour Guide hesitated, allowing a coy smile to tremble on her lips for a moment before answering, and Jill realized the woman went through this same spiel several times a day whenever the house, still a private residence, was open for tours. *What would she have done if I hadn't asked?* she wondered. No doubt she would have had a backup plan. Even so, Jill didn't regret playing into the woman's hands, for her curiosity was genuinely roused.

"Let's just say some of the details don't quite fit," Katherine said at last, having strung the suspense out until even the most avid photographer in the group had stopped clicking. "The needlework was certainly done by the duchess—you can see her initials stitched into the lower right-hand corner—but the timing is wrong, for one thing. It's true that the eighth duke was deeply in debt at the turn of the nineteenth century, but by the time his son assumed the title, the family was solvent once again. In fact, he made numerous improvements to the estate that his father could never have afforded. Now, as we enter this next room, you can see . . ."

Jill kept to the rear of the group as they shuffled after their guide. As she reached the door, however, she didn't pass through into the next room, but ducked back for a closer look at the framed needlework above the mantel. She found the light brown spots Katherine had described—too faint to see from a distance, especially when that distance had been filled with three generations of an American family in matching T-shirts, as well as a Japanese tourist with a camera as big as his head—and touched her finger to the museum-quality glass protecting the two-hundred-year-old fibers from, well, from people like her, who couldn't keep their hands to themselves.

"If only you could talk, what secrets could you tell?" she murmured aloud.

"Probably 'Please stay with your tour group,' " suggested an amused masculine voice somewhere behind her.

She spun around, and found a man regarding her quizzically, a very good-looking man in his late twenties, with bright green eyes and one blond curl drooping over his high forehead. She felt a sudden impulse to brush it back. Instead, she merely said, "Pot, meet kettle."

He laughed and shook his head. "I'm not with the group."

"Lucky you! Katherine the Tour Guide seems determined to rob it of any romance."

"Don't tell me, let me guess." His gaze shifted from Jill to the needlework and back again. "The bloodstains, right?"

"You know something about the family, then?"

He inclined his head in acknowledgement. "A little."

"What do you think about it, then? The legend, I mean, not the family."

He considered the matter as he crossed the room to stand next to her before the fireplace. "Most legends have some basis in fact. It's true that the duchess was originally from Lancashire, not far from a cotton mill that was owned by the husband of the duke's sister, so it's quite possible that the duke might have visited the area at some point, perhaps even met his future duchess there." He glanced back up at the framed piece over the mantel. "As for where this fits in—if it fits in at all—I'm afraid that part is lost to history."

"It's a shame, really. That's the part of history that

intrigues me—not what a few famous dead men did, but the daily lives of ordinary people."

He grinned broadly, exposing a dimple in his left cheek. "That's the first time I've ever heard of a duke being referred to as an 'ordinary' person."

"You know what I mean," she said with a little huff of annoyance.

"Strangely enough, I do. Are you a historian, then?"

She shook her head. "Not in the sense you mean. I did try to trace my family tree—my father's, that is, which sounds awfully sexist these days, but there's something so—so *constant* about the surname, don't you think? However much the world may change, that name continues on, from one generation to the next."

"Did you have any luck in your search?"

"Yes—and no. You can't believe half of what you see on those 'find your ancestors' websites, you know, but I did manage to trace it back two hundred years before hitting a brick wall."

"A lot can happen in two hundred years," he remarked. "Did you find anything interesting?"

"Nothing like this." She made a little wave of her hand that took in the Georgian house and all its furnishings. "I found a branch of the family in Australia, of all places, and one ancestor—the one from two hundred years ago—who married an aristocratic woman suspected of stabbing her husband to death. Her first husband, that is, not my great-great-whatever-great grandfather."

"Do tell!"

245

"I first found a mention of it on a genealogy website, but in this case, there was plenty of corroborating evidence: old *Times* articles that have been digitally preserved, as well as illustrations. They seem to have been parodied by all the famous caricaturists of their day. I even found a print for sale at an old book shop in Portobello Road. The thing cost thirty pounds, but I bought it and framed it, and now it's hanging in my kitchen."

"Right over the drawer where you keep your carving knives," he said, drawing the flat of his hand across his throat in a menacing gesture.

"Very funny," she retorted, laughing all the same. "Someone else was hanged for the murder, though, and according to the *Times*, my ancestor was the one who identified the real killer. In any case, they were married less than a year later. It must have been quite a scandal at the time, not only the fact that she married again so quickly, but that her second husband was so far beneath her socially."

"Intriguing," he remarked. "Do you suppose he coerced her? You know, 'I kept you from hanging for murder, now marry me or else I'll spill the beans about that blood-soaked glove at the bottom of your bureau drawer.' "

She gave him a skeptical look. "I suppose it's always possible, but considering that they had no fewer than six children, it seems unlikely."

"Did you uncover some connection to the Duke of Reddington, then? Is that what brought you here today?"

"No. That is," she amended, looking somewhat sheepish, "only a very minor connection. I guess you could say I'm a bit player in an uncredited role. In fact, a mutual friend set me up on a blind date with Lord Tisdale, the heir apparent—or do I mean heir presumptive? I always get those terms confused—and I wanted to learn what I could about the family. I mean, what do you say to the heir to a dukedom? My own family is hardly standing in the soup line, but we've got nothing like *this!*" Her wide-eyed gaze swept the room, taking in almost a thousand years of family history.

"First, 'heir apparent' is the term you want; it's *apparent* that Tisdale will inherit the dukedom from his father, as he's the eldest son. It's 'heir presumptive' when one *presumes* no one will be born who might knock him out of the succession. Second, you talk to the heir of a dukedom about the same things you might talk to anyone else about. Third, your family may not boast any dukes, but you have an ancestress who was almost tried for murder, which is something the Reddingtons can't claim."

Something about his tone and the knowing smile on his face gave Jill to understand that she had made rather a fool of herself. "Oh, God," she breathed, wishing the three-hundred-year-old floor might open up and swallow her. "You're him, aren't you? You're Lord Tisdale. The heir apparent."

"I'm Tisdale, yes, but you can call me Richard," he said, offering his hand. "And you must be Jill—"

She took his hand, and his fingers closed around hers, warm and strong. "Pickett," she said. "Jill Pickett."

About the Author

At the age of sixteen, Sheri Cobb South discovered Georgette Heyer, and came to the startling realization that she had been born into the wrong century. Although she probably would have been a chambermaid had she actually lived in Regency England, that didn't stop her from fantasizing about waltzing the night away in the arms of a handsome, wealthy, and titled gentleman.

Since Georgette Heyer died in 1974 and could not write any more Regencies, Ms. South came to the conclusion she would have to do it herself. After finishing *The Weaver Takes a Wife* and its two sequels (*Brighton Honeymoon* and *French Leave*), she'd thought she was done with these characters, until Lady 'elen's younger brother started insisting that his story be told. In addition to the "Weaver" books, she has also written several stand-alone Regency romances, as well as the bestselling John Pickett mysteries (referenced in the epilogue you've just read), now an award-winning audiobook series.

A native and long-time resident of Alabama, Ms. South now lives in Loveland, Colorado. And she loves to hear from readers! Look for her on social media:

Official website: www.shericobbsouth.com
Facebook: www.facebook.com/SheriCobbSouth
Twitter: @shericobbsouth
Instagram: sheri.cobb.south
Pinterest: www.pinterest.com/cobbsouth
or email her at Cobbsouth@aol.com

Made in the USA
Middletown, DE
17 August 2020